A Home For Christmas
Home for Christmas Series
Novella

Blue Saffire

Perceptive Illusions Publishing, Inc.
Bay Shore, New York

Blue Saffire/Perceptive Illusions Publishing, Inc.
PO BOX 5253
Bay Shore, New York 11706
www.BlueSaffire.com

Publisher's Note: This is a work of fiction. Names, characters, places, and incidents are a product of the author's imagination. Locales and public names are sometimes used for atmospheric purposes. Any resemblance to actual people, living or dead, or to businesses, companies, events, institutions, or locales is completely coincidental.

Ordering Information:
Quantity sales. Special discounts are available on quantity purchases by corporations, associations, and others. For details, contact the "Special Sales Department" at the address above.

A Home for Christmas: Home For Christmas Series Novella/ Blue Saffire. – 1st ed.
ISBN 978-1-941924-51-8

To be stripped bare is a burden wished upon no one. To find the silver lining after being stripped down to the bone is something I prayed for all.

—Blue Saffire

CHAPTER ONE

#

Tired

Allison

I'm truly exhausted. I should have slept at the hospital, but I just wanted away from that place for the two days I have off. God, I can't remember the last time I had a day off.

At least, it feels like I haven't had one in years. It doesn't help that the ER was a madhouse tonight. It was one of the worst Halloweens ever. It astonishes me how much people don't think.

"Just keep your eyes open," I murmur to myself.

I haven't made it out of the city yet. I dropped one of the nurses off in the projects up here. She's a sweet older lady. I hate knowing she has such a long commute after the hours she works. Driving her cuts her time by more than half.

It's not that far out of my way. Although, I have a much longer way to go. Lord, how am I going to make it all the way to Long Island? It's nights like this that I question my own sanity.

I could've gotten an apartment in Brooklyn or Queens. Heck, I'm to the point where I can afford a place in Manhattan. Yet, I love my small hometown. My family is so important to me.

It's never been a serious thought to leave them behind. Two more weeks. In two weeks, I'll be taking a leave. My mentor, Dr. Tucker, wants me to spend some time around her practice.

Correction, she wants me to take over her Long Island practice. I'm thirty, I'm single, I should be jumping all over this opportunity, but I'm just not sure. This leave is going to allow me to make some important decisions in my life.

While I've been building a career, all of my friends have been out living their lives, having fun, and getting married. I've had one serious relationship in the last ten years. Outside of that, my love life has been nonexistent.

"Shit," I mutter as my lids droop and I veer to the right.

I can't stop here. Not to take a nap. This is not a neighborhood you sleep in. I chose to work in Harlem. It was among my first picks for my residency. I thought I'd be making a difference having my brown face in a white coat.

Nights like this, I question whether I've made a difference at all. My surgical residency has been stellar. Yet, I'm not recognized for the work I've done. Others that are not black or female do half the work I do and have been promoted or given opportunities I've been overlooked for.

Another reason Dr. Tucker thinks it's time for me to make some changes. Being a trauma surgeon just doesn't speak to my heart the way it used to. Coming to the end of my residency has proven such.

Tonight was just one of the nails in the coffin. I'm a trauma surgeon. Yet, I was asked to man the ER this evening. Not that I mind stepping in to help wherever I can.

The problem is there were other doctors that could have and should have been assigned the ER before me. I'm one of the most skilled surgeons.

I don't think it would have bothered me so much if I didn't have to watch others get preferential treatment. I've held my tongue for the most part, but I'm just tired of it. It's why I didn't stick around to rest a bit before taking off.

"Crap," I murmur, rolling down the windows.

Just thinking about it all makes me tired. My body aches for my bed. I plan to sleep for a day and a half at least. I'm going to lose it if they decide to call me in.

Two weeks. Just two more weeks, Allison.

My car starts to swerve again. I can't do this. This is as bad as driving drunk. I need to pull over.

Just for ten minutes.

I should be able to make the drive if I rest my eyes for a few minutes. I pull over under an overpass. Still not the safest or best place, but I don't think I'm going to make it any further.

I barely shift the car into park properly. My lids start to droop as I roll the windows back up and push my head back against the rest. I recline the seat to get a little more comfortable, fading out before I can have another thought.

-B-

Roark

"Son of a bitch," I grumble out.

I can see my breath in front of me as the words float out. It would be a cold night. Just my luck. I tighten my thin jacket around me.

Five years, five fucking years. I lost five years of my life for a piece of shit. My step-brother from my mother's second marriage is a scumbag.

I lost everything trying to be loyal. Loyal to what? I don't even know anymore. What I do know is, thirty-one was too damn old to be going to jail for my fucked up little step-brother.

"Of all the stupid shit I've ever done," I mutter to myself.

This is how that piece of shit repays me. Ruined my business, allowed my home to be foreclosed on, and ran off with the money I had stashed away. I'm homeless. A real-life vagabond.

I've been going from shelter to shelter for over a month now. Honestly, I couldn't tell you how long it's been. Tonight, I didn't even get in. I've been looking for work, but my record isn't helping that effort move in the right direction.

Now, as I look back on things, I should have thought about what I was doing for Carter. The kid needed to learn a lesson. Some hard time probably would have been in his best interest.

However, I thought being that I didn't have any priors and I was a good standing member of my community, I would get off with a slap on the wrist. I would have if I was only being charged for the assault. I had no idea Carter had a gun and drugs stashed in my car.

I let him run off to cover his ass and I was left holding a fucked up bag. I will regret that day for the rest of my life. My barbershops are gone. I can't reinstate my license because of the nature of my convictions.

My shitty lawyer should have gotten me off, but the prosecutor had a hard-on for me and my lawyer didn't seem to care. My tattoos and piercings made me guilty, nothing else. I never should've taken my ass to the city that night.

Out on the Island, everyone knows everyone. There was no way I was getting locked up for anything in my hometown. Even if it were a county over, someone would have vouched for me.

My mom's third husband did so much for me. I owed Henry so much. He kept my nose clean and made me want to be something—someone.

Which is why there's no reason for me to be sitting here under this trestle, starving and freezing my ass off. Losing my mom and step-father was hard on me. It's the reason I got caught up with Carter. I wasn't thinking straight because I was still grieving.

That shit still hurts. I feel my eyes burn with tears I'll never shed. How does life just fall apart like this? I feel like I just keep getting shitted on over and over again.

Laughter and jeers pull me from my thoughts. Only trouble would be out here on these streets this time of night. I see the group of young punks wasting their lives away.

They're looking to steal a car. I know the MO. The Mercedes from earlier catches my attention again. I don't know why it keeps drawing me in. Maybe because it sticks out under here like a sore thumb.

My eyes narrow as I see something or should I say someone shifting inside. My hackles rise. The group of guys is nearing the car. If jail taught me nothing else, it taught me to keep my head down and mind my own business.

I plan to do just that. That is until I see the female that sits up inside the vehicle. By now, the car is surrounded. Their laughter increases with their excitement of an easy find.

A woman in an expensive car with the keys. They've hit a payday. Again, I tell myself to mind my business.

Yet, I'm on my feet. The cold weather is forgotten as an eerie chill runs through my bones. I'm not about to watch this woman get carjacked by five guys.

"Open the door, bitch." One of the guys demands.

"Don't make us break the windows." One of the other two now standing in front of the car threatens.

"She's fine as fuck too." The guy at the rear of the car says.

"Back off," I bark as I get closer.

All heads turn toward me. At six three, I tower over most of them. However, I'm two hundred lean since living on the streets. Maybe less. I'm probably not as intimidating as I think I am in my head.

"White boy, you better go about your dirty ass way. You don't want this smoke, son. Mind your fucking business," the one on the driver's side hollers back.

"Word." One of the others cosigns.

"Listen, it's cold out. Leave the lady alone and find something else to do. You don't have little brothers and sisters at home with candy you should be sorting for them?" I respond.

"Will you listen to this motherfucker?" The one with the most mouth says.

He pulls a gun and I feel the situation shift. He aims the gun at my chest with a smile on his lips. Little does he know, I don't have a thing left to live for.

"Now, that's what I'm talking about." One of the others croons.

"You sure you want to do that? I'm just coming off a five-year bid. That's not a life you want," I say calmly.

"So what? You think you're hard or something because you did some time? I'm going to tell you one more time, go mind your business." He says cocking the gun.

"Oh my God, please stop," a female voice calls out. "I've called the police. Just go."

I shift my gaze to see she has lowered the lightly tinted window enough to be heard, but she's still inside. Good. I need her to stay right where she is.

"The cops ain't coming out here," he snorts. "You might as well get out of the car, ma. You and your dirty boyfriend can wait to see how long it takes for them to show up."

His friends laugh around the car. It's in that split second that he turns his head to show off that I make a decision. Knocking the gun from his hands, I toss my palm into his throat.

In my mind, once I have the guys' attention on jumping me, the woman in the car will be able to drive away. What happens is something totally different. When the other four round the car to jump me, I don't go down without a fight.

Adrenaline and the alcohol that's been warming my blood courses through my veins. I've needed an outlet for this anger for an entire month. Since the day I was released from jail and found out Carter left my ass without a life.

I've been good with my hands for a long time. My mom took me to box to get out some of my earlier aggression as a preteen going into my teens. I had a hard time as she moved through her first two marriages.

I can say the golden gloves saved my life back then. It's not doing a bad job now. That is until the loud bang that rings out and the searing pain that pierces my side.

I'm knocked to the ground by the force of the blow. My left-hand goes to my side. I pull my fingers away to find them soaked in my blood.

"Oh, shit! You shot him, son. I'm out." One of the guys calls out nervously.

"What about the car?" Another asks.

"Fuck the car. I'm not going down for a body, B. I'm out," the first replies.

I hear their footfalls as they run away. I haven't taken my eyes off of my bleeding hand. This is how my life ends? Two dollars in my pocket. No place to call home, dirty, and in the middle of the street.

All because I'm always saving someone. My one hope... I hope this woman deserves my life, unlike my undeserving step-brother.

CHAPTER TWO

Forever Grateful

Allison

So much for sleeping away my two days off. I've been here by my hero's side since I performed the surgery that saved his life. My colleagues must think I'm crazy. I was adamant that I would be the one to save him.

I wasn't taking no for an answer. After watching him fight for me, I knew I had to be the one. My fatigue was forgotten as I retrieved the bullet that was floating in his body.

He was lucky. I got to the bullet before any major organs could be damaged. If I left him in the hands of one of my colleagues, that bullet would still be swimming inside of him, able to do more damage.

I'm not a fan of the wait and see method the hospital has employed. My decision was well worth the suspension. I just found out three hours ago that I'm being suspended without pay until my leave.

I cheesed off a lot of people performing surgery on a homeless man. For this homeless man, I'd do it again. Waking up disoriented in my car to find it surrounded, scared the shit out of me.

So many thoughts ran through my head. I didn't know what to do. At first, I didn't know what distracted them from knocking on my windows. Then I saw the homeless guy arguing with them on my behalf.

I'd never been more scared in my life than when the guy that was shaking the handle of my driver's side door pulled that gun. Here this homeless man was, trying to help me and he was being held at gunpoint. It all happened so fast.

Him knocking the gun from the young guy's hands, the others rushing him to jump him. The homeless guy knocking one of them out, while fighting off the others.

I was in shock as I sat there watching it all unfold. He moved so fluidly, fighting as if he were trained to do so. For such a tall guy, he still handles his lean body well.

Then the shot rang out. I can still hear it two entire days later. Since the adrenaline has worn off, I've been a nervous wreck. I walked out of that OR and fell apart. Exhausted, drained, and frazzled—I stood and cried with gratitude for my life.

The car could have been replaced. I was never concerned about it. I was worried about what else they may have decided they wanted once I relinquished the vehicle.

This man saved my life. He stepped in and placed his life on the line for me. I will forever be grateful for that.

"Allison. Thank, God."

I look up to see my mother rushing into the room. I called my parents and sisters to let them know what had happened. They were all concerned about me. I should've known my mother would show up.

My sisters, India and Erica, follow behind my mother. I roll my eyes. They didn't all have to come up here. I know the only reason my father isn't with them is because he's away on business.

"Mom, what are you doing here?"

"You think you can call me and tell me that you were held at gunpoint and almost carjacked and I'm just going to sit at home, twiddling my thumbs." She says as she pulls me up from my chair and wraps me in a hug.

"I was not held at gunpoint," I grumble.

"That's not what you said on the phone," she replies.

"Yes, it is. I told you the guy that saved my life was held at gunpoint. Not me."

"Same thing to me," she says.

"Is that him?" India whispers.

"Yeah." I nod and swallow.

India squints her eyes as she peers over at him. Erica creeps over to his side. I shake my head at my sisters.

"He looks familiar," India mutters to herself, pursing her lips in thought.

"I know, right?" Erica says thoughtfully.

"Get over here." I hiss at my youngest sister, Erica.

"What?" She blinks her big eyes at me.

She walks over and I wrap an arm around her shoulders. I kiss the side of my sister's head. Erica has been struggling with her health for years. It's good to see her looking well today.

My sisters have been through so much. It has all made them stronger. I've had a lot of time to think about my family while sitting here.

I feel like I haven't been there for them as much as they've needed me to be. Being a surgeon has become everything. It's one of the reasons I've never moved from our hometown. I felt like if I did, I'd be totally disconnected from our family unit.

"I'm glad to see you guys," I admit.

"You scared the crap out of us," India says.

I shiver. "I still can't believe it."

"You have to explain to me what the heck happened." My mother demands.

"I will," I say on a sigh. "Let's take a walk. I've been sitting too long."

"You're sure you want to leave?" India says, her eyes dancing over my face.

No, I don't, but I need to get some air. He's not going to be lucid anytime soon. We've been keeping him heavily medicated for the pain.

Those blue eyes have opened a few times, but he goes right back to sleep. He was severely dehydrated and undernourished. It will take him a little longer to recover, but he's going to be okay.

"Yeah, come on. I miss you guys." I reply.

-B-

Roark

I feel nothing but pain as I open my eyes. I wait for them to adjust to the dim lighting. Sensing someone in the room, I turn my head to the right.

The first thing to capture my attention is her hair. It's short and sassy. Those are the first words to come to mind. The sides are combed into large finger waves and the top is piled high with curls.

It's the perfect cut for her heart-shaped face. It opens up the view of those big brown eyes, her cute nose, and those sexy as fuck lips. Her skin is perfection against her dark hair. That singer Fantasia comes to mind. Only, I think this beauty sitting before me may be a few shades darker.

A stunner.

There's no other way to describe her. She's watching me closely as I take her in. My brows crease as my brain starts to catch up. My mouth is moving before my thoughts click into place.

"Allison?"

Her brows mirror mine as the name floats out. From the look on her face, I know I have it right. You don't forget the name of a woman like this one.

"How do you know my na... You know me?" she replies in confusion.

Licking my dry lips, I try to swallow past the lump in my throat. It feels like sandpaper was stuffed down the passage. Nothing feels right. My side is itching, but my arms feel too heavy to reach for the spot to scratch.

"Wait, don't talk," she commands, getting up from her seat.

Pouring a glass of water for me, she places a straw in the cup and brings it to my mouth. Our eyes lock as I take the straw between my chapped lips.

I look away. Her eyes should be considered the eighth wonder of the world. I remember the first time she captured me in them.

My mind works, trying to figure out where I am and how I got here. My brain tingles with the information standing before me. The terrible lighting, the rough blankets, the beeping sound, and Allison—she's a doctor, no a surgeon.

It starts to come back to me. I was shot. I tried to play the hero and I was gunned down. I'm starting to think that's a misguided trait of mine. I help and I get burned.

My brows draw. I remember Allison's face hovering over me as I bled out. I remember thinking I actually made it to heaven. Only angels are so beautiful you forget the pain of a slug burning through your gut.

"Is she okay?" I ask, still disoriented, trying to make sense of my jumbled up thoughts.

"Who?" Allison replies, her brows pulled together on the center of her pretty face.

"The woman in the car," I push out through my hoarse voice.

Her brows smooth out and her eyes soften. If it's possible, she just became more beautiful with the smile that takes over her face. She places the straw back to my lips and I take it.

"I was the one in the car. You saved my life. I'll never be able to repay you for what you did for me," she says softly.

I start to choke on the water. My right-hand goes limply to my left side. Wincing through the pain, I gasp in a breath.

"What were you doing, sitting in your car in that neighborhood?"

"I just needed to close my eyes for a bit. I was exhausted and the drive home is so long," she cuts off, tugging that full bottom lip between her teeth.

"Were you hurt?"

"No, but you were lucky I was there," she replies.

Her eyes narrow, gaze sharpening on my face. I must look like shit. Lifting my hand, I touch my beard. For the last month of my life, I've been the most unkept ever.

I got into grooming and became a barber because I pride myself on looking clean and I love the artistic side of it. I remember the first shop I worked at. I had to earn my stripes.

A white boy cutting in a black shop. The jokes went on for days until I got my shot. My stepfather asked a friend of his to stop by and get a cut from me. The friend happened to be a young NBA player that purchased a couple of custom cars from my step-father.

I put my all into that fade. He left with a shape up so sharp he started to come see me whenever he was in town. After a while, I started traveling to cut for him and his teammates. That led to me opening my first shop.

I owe so much to my stepfather. My eyes drop. He would be so disappointed to see me like this. I worked hard for my dreams and this is not what he would have wanted for me.

"I guess we were both lucky tonight," I murmur.

"Oh, it's been a few nights since the incident. It's been two days." She says cautiously.

I close my eyes and nod. I feel like a truck hit me. I'm not surprised I've been out of it for two days.

"Earlier, you called me by my name. Do you know me?"

"It's a small world." I give a dry chuckle.

When I open my eyes, she's staring back at me. This time I hold her gaze. I'm not surprised she doesn't recognize me. I'm not sure I want her to. I'd prefer if she'd turn around and walk away.

Her brows thread so deeply, they make a little crease in her forehead. Her eyes begin to bounce around my face. I hold my breath as I wait for her to make the connection.

"I'm sorry. I—"

Her words are cut off by a knock on the door. Both of our heads swing to the interruption. Two officers are standing at the door. Their badges resting on their chests.

My hackles go up. I don't have the best relationship with the NYPD. Since taking the rap for Carter, I'm not a fan of the New York City system.

Say what you want about Long Island. The law enforcement has a different culture in my old county. Most times the guys on the force just want to make it through their shift and return home to their families. They're not out to give you a hard time or make a name for themselves in a big pool of fish. Not like NYPD.

"We were hoping the patient was up. Happened to be here for another case. Thought we'd stop in to see if we could ask a few questions." One of the ununiformed officers says.

"Hey, guys. He's only been up for a little bit. Maybe you should come back after someone can come in and evaluate him," Allison says.

Her tone has a familiarity as if she knows these guys. The tall one with the dark hair that hasn't spoken, has his eyes locked on her with a smile in the corner of his lips. My jaw tightens as jealousy courses through me.

"It's fine. We can get this over with." I grumble.

She turns to me, reaching to touch my arm. Her eyes are assessing, but this time she's not searching to make a connection. She's looking to see something else.

"Are you sure?"

"Yeah, it's fine." I nod.

"Here, have some more water." She says, lifting the straw back to my lips.

"I told you guys what happened. Can't you give him some more time to heal," she protests despite my agreement.

"It's best if we get the details while they're as fresh as possible." The shorter officer says.

"Dr. Myers, do you think I can talk to you for a minute?" The other officer speaks up.

Allison looks between the two of us indecisively. The look on her face says she doesn't want to leave my side. She has a protective air about her.

Placing the cup down, she looks me over one more time. I can see she's still torn about whether she wants to leave or not. I give her a reassuring nod.

"I'll have someone come in to check on you," she says to me, causing my brows to draw. She turns to the officers. "Don't push him too hard."

I watch in confusion as she leaves the room. I'm not understanding why she needs someone else to come to check on me. It dawns on me that I truly don't remember what kind of doctor or surgeon she is. Yet, she said I was lucky she was there.

Was she not the one that saved my life?

I watch her move towards the door, looking back over her shoulder at me when she reaches the tall officer. My lips tighten when I watch him place a hand on her back to lead her out of the room. She turns to look up at him, then follows him out.

"Can you tell me what you were doing at the scene of the crime that night?"

My attention is pulled to the officer that has moved to the side of my bed. Here we go. I'm going to be treated like the criminal, not the victim with the gunshot wound.

-B-

Allison

"I think you should be careful with that guy. I can see you're getting attached. I know he saved your life, but you don't know anything about him." Detective Dawson Green warns.

"I'll be fine," I say, rolling my eyes.

Dawson can be a little bit overprotective when it comes to me. Being a trauma surgeon has placed me on a first name basis with a few officers. Dawson, however, has become a friend. I know he would like to be more than friends but I've never felt that spark with him.

He's just not my type. That hasn't stopped him from asking me out repeatedly. I don't know if he thinks I'm going to magically change my mind or something.

"We found his backpack with his ID at the scene. A jail ID. He's an ex-con, Allison. Fresh out. He was just released a few months ago. I want you to stay away from him." Dawson says more firmly.

My head whips back. Surely, I'm hearing things wrong. Maybe my fatigue is setting in because I know he can't be seriously using that tone with me.

"First of all, Dawson. Last time I checked, my father isn't an NYPD detective. I can interact with whoever I want." I hiss.

"You don't know this guy. You've already been suspended because of him," he retorts.

Again, my head jerks back. I know rumors and gossip get around in this hospital but I wasn't expecting him to have this knowledge. I'm beyond pissed off now.

"How do you know that?"

"I have my sources," he mutters.

"Yeah, whatever," I reply, moving to push past him to reenter the room.

I want them to get out and leave him alone. He saved my life. I could tell by the way they walked into the room that they were there to bust his chops. Not on my watch.

"Allison," Dawson growls while grabbing a hold of my arm.

I turn to look at his hand in warning. I stare at it, then move my eyes to his face. His lips are pursed and his eyes are hard.

"It's Dr. Myers and I think you want to take your hand off of me." I snap.

He sighs, releasing my arm but stepping in to crowd my space. I don't like it, but I don't back up. Instead, I fold my arms over my chest and stand my ground.

"You've been in this hospital by his side for days. I get it. You feel indebted to him for saving your life. Fine. But I'm telling you. He's bad news. Be careful." He warns.

"The fact that you know I've been by his side both disturbs and pisses me off. I'm not your responsibility. You don't have to check up on me." I return.

This isn't the first time I'm finding out that he's been snooping around to find out things about me. The first few times, I thought it was cute. A guy with a crush or something. Now, I'm just hotter than fish grease.

"Allison—"

"No," I hold up my hand. "We're done here. Get your partner and leave."

I turn from going to enter the room to go find someone to tend to the man that saved my life. I've had enough of this conversation and I need to calm down before I go back in there.

The nerve of some people.

CHAPTER THREE

The Offer

Roark

The hospital food hasn't been the greatest, but it's been more than I've had in weeks. I'm not looking forward to being released in the morning. I haven't figured out what my next move is.

Now that I'm injured that's going to make finding work harder than it already was. This shit show just keeps getting better. I can't seem to catch a break.

"Shit," I grunt.

A loud groan follows as I shift in the bed to get more comfortable. I'm not going to complain about this bed. It's the best I've had in five years and that's saying a lot.

I stare off into space as I remember the days when I had a king-sized bed to go home to. I bought my first home in

Smithtown, Long Island when I was twenty-five. My parents wanted to help, but it was something I wanted to do on my own.

I was proud of that place. It wasn't the biggest house because of the side of town I wanted to live on. It was what I could afford, which was still pretty damn decent.

"I wish you could see the look on your face," Allison's voice grabs my attention.

I remain silent. I've been trying to keep my distance. It's not lost on me that everyone seems to be concerned with how much Allison is here. From the other doctors and nurses to those cops.

I don't blame them for wanting to look out for her, but it still stings that everyone has made assumptions about me. After all, I am the man that put his life in danger to save someone else's.

"Are you excited to be getting out of here?" She says when I don't respond.

"Not really. It's not like I have big plans." I mumble the first words I've said to her since those officers arrived yesterday.

"I'm sorry that was insensitive of me," she says, her voice sounding hopeful as I return her words. "I'm glad you're talking, by the way. What do you say we work on those plans? Do you have family I can reach out to for you? Friends maybe?"

I turn to look into her concerned eyes. I have a hard time ignoring that pretty face. To think, she doesn't even remember me. Not that I blame her. I don't recognize me anymore.

"Anyone that would care about what happens to me is long gone, sweetheart. But thanks."

"Where will you go?"

"Back to the streets. I'll get into a shelter when I can, but I'm probably better off on the streets until I can heal," I reply.

"What?" Her face compresses.

"It gets rough in some of the shelters," I say simply.

I can see the wheels spinning in her head. I turn back toward the TV. If I place my focus on it, I don't have to worry about the pity I see in her eyes.

Allison Myers is the last person I wanted to see me like this. I thought I wasn't good enough back then. I know I'm not now. All of the twists and turns my life has taken, have led me to be half the man I was when I decided not to overplay my hand with her.

"There has to be someth—"

"I'll be fine," I say, closing the subject.

~B~

Allison

He's finally talking to me, but he isn't behaving very friendly. It would piss me off under different circumstances but I think I understand. He doesn't have a place to live or people to help him.

Not to mention, he has been treated like a criminal, not the hero turned victim that he is. I'm still steaming about Dawson's visit and it's an entire day later. The man sitting before me hasn't spoken to me since.

I still want to help him. It's the least I can do. His medical stay has been taken care of by my family. My dad offered to help any way he could. Daddy also wanted to raise hell about my suspension, but I talked him off the ledge.

"You know, I have enough room at my place. There's only me. It's not a huge place, but I do have an extra bedroom," the words are out of my mouth before I think them through.

He turns his blue eyes on me again. Something flashes in them, but I don't catch it fast enough to pin it down. Although,

I'm not alarmed. I haven't gotten a single bad vibe from him. Even with his silence.

"You would invite some stranger into your home. You clearly don't know me," he says.

I sense a bit of bitterness in his words. At least, it seems like I do. Something about that nags at me. I can't help but feel like I should know him. I never did get an answer to my question.

"You need someplace to stay. At least until you heal properly. Maybe even until you can find a way to get on your feet," I reply.

Somewhere between finding out he has no one and making the offer, my mind has been made up. I'm going to make sure he has shelter.

"If you don't feel comfortable at my place, maybe I can pool my resources to find you other accommodations after a few days," I continue.

"Thanks for the offer, but I don't have anything to contribute to earn my keep," he says.

"I didn't ask you for anything."

"I don't think it's a good idea," he says, turning from me again.

"You have a better idea." I huff, folding my arms over my chest.

"Why are you here? I'm breathing. You saved my life. I think that makes us even. You don't have to worry about me anymore. I'll figure it out," he says, his jaw tightening.

I take a step back. I wasn't expecting that reaction. My head drops. I start to think as I smooth my hands down my shirt.

"I'm just trying to help. But if you're—"

"I'm sorry," he releases a heavy sigh. "Listen, no one has given a shit about me in years. You're sweet and so is your offer, but you don't know a thing about me."

"I know you were kind enough to take a bullet for me. That's enough for me at the moment. I don't live here in the city, but I have a nice place out on the Island. I have tons of food because I'm never home. Since my leave is starting earlier than I planned, I have time to help you. Let me. You can stay with me until after Christmas. I'll feel comfortable with you going on your way then," I reply.

Something shifts in his eyes as his jaw works. I can see an internal war happening. I don't realize I'm holding my breath until he speaks again.

"It will only be until I can move around and get out of your way. Which, I plan to do as soon as I can," he says quietly.

"Christmas. That will be the proper time to heal internally."

He frowns but I see him leaning towards a yes. I watch as the gears turn. I'm offering him the best option.

"Okay, Christmas, but if I feel better before then—"

"I'm the doctor. I know what's best." I say with a smile.

"Yeah, sure."

"I guess I should probably go home and set up your room."

"You don't have to go through any trouble for me," he says.

"It's no trouble at all. Rest up. I'll be back in the morning," I say, patting his arm.

I turn to grab my things and leave. In all honesty, I've run out of scrubs in my locker. I need to go home, shower and pull myself together.

CHAPTER FOUR

A New Man

Allison

I don't know why I'm so nervous. It's not like my house is some dump or dirty or anything. I purchased the little home a few years ago, with hopes to use it as an investment property in a year or two.

I'm hardly ever home. When I am, I'm usually sleeping off my shifts. However, something about allowing this man into my house has me feeling like I need to explain why it's so neat and looks unlived in.

It looks more like a staged home than someplace someone lives. I wouldn't call myself a neat freak. I honestly just am never here.

"This is a really nice place," he murmurs beside me.

"Thanks," I reply. "There's a bathroom next door to your bedroom. I placed a grooming kit in there. Not saying you need to clean yourself up or anything…I…I just got you a few things just in case."

My words rush out as my face and ears flame. If it weren't for my chocolate skin, I'd probably be bright red. I've been sticking my foot in my mouth all morning.

"Don't worry about it. I wouldn't mind a shave and cut," he says with a chuckle.

The sound relaxes me and brings a smile to my face. He's a handsome man under all of that shoulder length hair and the overgrown beard, but I have wondered what he looks like without it. I shouldn't care, but I'm curious.

"I can take you to a barbershop or spa if you'd like," I say without thinking.

"Nah, sweetheart. I don't need to be in anyone's spa and the shops around here suck," he says.

My brows bunch. I wonder how he would know about the shops in this neighborhood. That's a pretty bold thing to assume.

My phone rings before I can comment. It's my mother. She's been calling non-stop the last few days. I roll my eyes and point in the direction of the bathroom for him to find it.

Heading into the kitchen to heat the chili I made last night, I answer the phone. I can't help inhaling deeply, stilling myself for what's to come. My parents have been overbearing since they found out about the attack.

"Hey, Mom," I say.

"Hey, your sister said she thought she passed you on the road. Did you finally go home and get some rest?"

"Yes, I did. I made something for dinner tonight and then had a full eight hours of sleep after that," I reply.

"Well, it's about time. I hope you plan to rest some more before running back to that hospital to sit at that boy's bedside."

I roll my eyes.

"Actually, he was released this morning," I say.

"Oh," I can hear the concern in her voice. "Well, did they help him find someplace to stay? Your father would have been more than happy to put him up in a room until he heals."

"He has a place. I took care of it."

"*Allison,*" she drags out. "What have you done now?"

"We'll talk about it later, Mom."

"Jesus, these girls are out to kill me," she says dramatically.

"Later, Mom," I chuckle and end the call.

While the chili is heating, I work to get the bread in the oven. A nice hot meal is just what the doctor ordered for my new guest. That doctor being me.

I plan to put some meat on those bones while he's with me. He was so malnourished when he entered the hospital, but I'm sure he'll fatten up after a few meals with me. After all, I'm here to get him healthy and back out into the world.

Dr. Myers to the rescue.

~B~

Roark

I've never been so happy to see a razor and clippers in my life. Allison did more than get me a simple grooming kit. I shake my head at the basket full of male hygiene products.

Nevertheless, I use them. I start with a shower, washing as best I can without soaking the bandages. It takes some effort and a lot of pain, but I make it work.

When I step out of the shower, I wrap a towel around my waist and look myself in the mirror. I look like shit. Although, I think I put a little weight back on since being in the hospital.

"Damn, Roark," I murmur to the reflection before me.

I need this hair off my face and a haircut I can stand to look at. Reaching for the Wahl clippers in the basket, I shake my head. These aren't cheap amateur clippers. She spent way too much money on me.

"I'll pay her back as soon as I figure my shit out," I huff to myself.

Placing the clippers down, I start with the shears. The sink is filled with my golden locks in no time. Retrieving the clippers again, I bring the old Roark back. I look half human once I have a low fade on the sides and a sharp shape up going.

Seeing the hair products in the basket, I think to try something new. Instead of bringing the top down to match the sides and back, I leave a few inches. Combing it all over, I shrug.

I work on the beard next. Same process. I shear the length off first, but I used the trimmers to give me a close neat beard. I don't know why I keep the facial hair. I normally shave it completely off, but it works as I look at my slimmer face. It gives the illusion that I have more weight on me than I do.

I take the little brush and groom my new look. It's the cleanest I've felt in five years. I can see me in there somewhere. I nod in satisfaction at the man in the mirror.

"Not bad, Roark," I say and give myself a wink.

I turn to the clothes I came here in. Allison offered me a pair of scrubs she found after realizing I didn't have shit to wear. I go to pick them up, but a knock sounds on the door.

"Yeah?" I reply to the tapping.

"I found some clothes for you," she says through the barrier.

Moving to the door, I crack it open. Allison's eyes go wide and her mouth falls open. Finally, the recognition I'd been expecting all this time appears.

"Ro," she chokes out.

"What's up, Allison?" I say with a crooked grin.

-B-

Allison

Oh my God. I had such a big crush on this man when I was younger. I mean huge. I don't know how it didn't click before this. In my defense, he was well hidden under all of that hair and grime.

But now, I see it. His blue eyes stand out in his handsome face. He has that sharp shape up like always, with the exception of the longer hair on top. It's not what I'm used to on him, but I like it. And those dimples. I can see them now with the neatly trimmed beard.

"I...I... Wow, I had no idea. Why didn't you say something?" I stammer out.

He shrugs his shoulders, drawing my eyes down to his tattoo-covered chest. Okay, looks like he has started to gain some weight back already. I shouldn't be checking him out in his towel but damn.

"I told you my name," he replies.

Ro. I can't believe this.

Yeah, he told me his name, but I didn't connect the dots. I've never known him by his full name. My brows thread.

"What happened to you?"

Ugh, where the hell is my filter? Why can't I keep my foot out of my mouth around him? I palm my forehead and groan.

When I look up again, his lips are pursed and so many emotions are in his eyes. I see hurt, embarrassment, anger, among a few other things. I feel like a jerk.

"Things change," he shrugs. "Those for me?"

He's pointing to the sweats and T-shirt I have in my hand. They belong to my little cousin. I just remembered they were here.

"Oh yeah," I say softly. Then I start to ramble. "I spoiled my little cousin when he was here for a while before going to college. I went overboard with shopping. He couldn't get it all into his bags. He had to leave some things behind. I was supposed to ship the rest to him, but I just never had the time and forgot eventually. But um, it worked out fine after all. "

"Yeah, thanks," he says holding out his hands.

I give over the items and our fingers brush as he takes them from me. Warmth blooms in my stomach and my skin is left tingling. I take a step back, feeling as if I've just been burned.

"I can change that bandage for you," I offer.

"Yeah, maybe later," he murmurs.

"Okay, as long as it's changed."

"I'll manage."

"Um, there's chili and some bread I baked, if you're hungry," I say, dropping my eyes to the floor.

"Smells good. I'll be out in a few," he says, closing the door and shutting me out.

"You have got to learn to shut up," I chastise myself as I walk back to my bedroom to lock myself in so I can scream into my pillow.

Only I would be saved by my crush and find out that he's homeless. I just don't understand. Ro had so much going for him. I admired his drive.

I mean, I don't know him know him. He's the cousin of the father of my sister's kids. However, Ro left an impression on me back in the day.

He was different from the guys I was used to. He had an easy swagger, and those eyes. I should have known from the eyes. In my defense, we only met a few times.

There was just that one party. That single night, where for just a moment, I thought we had a connection. At least, until I watched him leave with someone else. I never saw him again after that.

"What are you going to do now?" I groan into my pillow.

~ B ~

Roark

I should probably leave. Now that she knows it's me, it might be the best thing to do. I never wanted anyone from home to see me like this. I've had enough of my pride crushed—being placed in cuffs and eventually an orange jumpsuit.

Yet, I've been sitting here for the last five minutes waiting for her to come back out here. My stomach growls for the umpteenth time. That chili smells more than amazing. I don't want to just help myself to anything in her home. I also don't want to be a bother.

Staring into my palms resting on the table before me with my fingers lock together, I play my life over and over. How did it all get so fucked up? I wanted something like this.

A girl as fine as Allison. A nice crib like this. Maybe even a couple of babies by now. I would have expanded the shops and been a brand.

Now, I can't even get my barber license back and my shops are gone. Rage burns my veins. This is my fault. Always looking out for others and not myself.

"Hey," Allison's voice pulls me from my thoughts.

I lift my head and look in her direction just as my stomach growls again. I wince on the inside, but the soft smile she gives me causes my entire body to relax.

"Why didn't you get yourself something to eat?" She says moving into the kitchen.

"I didn't want to take liberties. I'm a guest," I reply.

"Oh please," she laughs. "As long as you're here, think of it as home. Anything you want, you're welcome to."

Does that include you?

Shit. See that's the reason I know I should leave. I'm still attracted to her. Maybe even more so. At about five six, maybe five seven, Allison has filled out a bit more since back when I first met her ten years ago. It looks good though. Really good.

I clear my throat. "Thanks."

It's lame but it's all I've got. Literally. I look around her house. It's picture perfect. I couldn't even fix some things for her if I wanted to. It looks like she has everything she needs.

I wonder if that includes a man.

My lips tighten. I need to bury those thoughts. She's a surgeon and I'm what? An ex-con. I hate that word. If I'd earned it I'd be good with that, but I haven't.

"You look like you have a lot on your mind. Want to talk about it?" She says as she places a bowl in front of me and a basket of bread on the table.

"Not really," I say before diving into the chili.

My eyes close and I groan. It's that good. I haven't had a home cooked meal in years. I'm shoveling spoonful in my mouth like I'm in the mess hall.

Reaching for the bread I rip a chunk off and start to dip it in the sauce. My head lifts when I feel her eyes on me. She's sitting with a bowl of her own. A smile is on that gorgeous face as always.

"Is it good?"

"Yeah, you might have some skills," I say, giving her a lopsided grin.

"Thanks," she says dipping her head shyly.

I remember that being one of the things that attracted me to her. She has this quiet intrigue about her that I like. I wanted to explore that until Carter told me who her family was and that she was destined to be a doctor.

I knew then she was out of my league. And that was before my life blew up in my face. The thought makes me force my attention back to my bowl.

"I want to thank you for all of this. I don't think I have. Thank you," I say as I stare down into my food.

"You're more than welcome. I want to help in any way I can," she replies.

"Why?"

The words float out before I can stop them. When I look up she's staring at me with her brows creased. Her eyes soften and she reaches across the table for one of my hands.

Sparks fly the moment she touches me. The lift of her brows tell me she feels it too. She doesn't remove her hand though.

"Some people just want to be helpful. I'm one of them. It's why I became a doctor. I want to help people. The fact that you helped me is an added incentive. I think now that I know you're family that's another reason," she says and shrugs.

"Family?" I say in confusion.

Her face pinches a little, bring a sour look to her features. She shifts in her seat a bit. I watch as she seems to war with her own thoughts.

"India…never mind. It's complicated and not my place to tell anyone," she says.

My interest is peaked, but I don't say anything. I lost touch with so many people when my life fell apart. Some just didn't care and some were too busy with their own lives to help me with mine.

"We can go out shopping tomorrow for more clothes. I'll need to get things for Thanksgiving dinner while I'm at it," she says.

"You don't have to do that. Wait…Thanksgiving?

"Yeah, I know there's still about two weeks to go, but I hate waiting until the last minute and being out in the chaos," she says.

"Damn, I've been on the streets that long," I say more to myself.

I stand. Now that I think about it, the night I was shot was Halloween, but it's just dawning on me how long it's been. My appetite suddenly vanishes. Reality setting in. I have nothing to be grateful for and haven't had anything in a very long time.

"I'm going to get some sleep," I say reaching for my bowl to clean after myself.

"Leave it. I'll take care of it. You can do the dishes tomorrow," she says with that sweet smile.

"All right. Good night," I reply and turn for the bedroom she pointed out as mine.

CHAPTER FIVE

Recovery

Roark

"Sit up," Allison says, as she stands in front of me with a basket and a bowl of popcorn in her hands.

My brows wrinkle as I look back at her. I've been here a few days now and I try my best not to lie around like some freeloader. Yet today, my body just feels like shit.

"Come on," she says when I don't move. "Sit up. It's raining out. I've seen you wincing a few times. Your body is reacting to the weather."

I lift up into a sitting position and a smile comes to her lips. She places the basket down on the couch and the popcorn in my lap. Reaching for my T-shirt, she pulls it over my head.

"Do you mind if I turn to the game? I mean, if you're watching this that's okay." She nods at the Christmas movie I put on, thinking she would want to watch it.

I drowned the sound out a long time ago. Her request for the game is welcomed. I give a shrug and hand over the remote.

"I wasn't watching this," I reply.

"Great," she says.

Turning to a football game, her face lights up. Damn, this girl is after my heart. If I had a thing for her before, I'm in love now. She's into football, she can cook her ass off, and she's smart and funny as hell.

She's a lethal combination. If I had my shit together I would totally go for her this time around. My face compresses with that thought. I still don't know what I'm going to do and my debts to her are only adding up.

She's given me food, shelter, and clothes. She went crazy with buying me clothes. I'm learning Allison does everything big.

"Do you want anything else?" she asks, nodding at the popcorn in my lap.

"Nah, I'm fine," I say.

She settles in beside me. Reaching for the oil inside of her basket. She pours some into her palms and she warms it in her hands. Shifting to her knees, she moves closer.

"Okay, now to work on these muscles," She says. "Turn to me, give me your back."

Her hands feel like heaven as they touch my shoulders and she begins to rub the oil in. I inhale a deep breath and allow the tension to release. Her slim fingers massage and dig out the knots and kinks.

"That feels amazing." I groan.

"You're stiff from not moving around much. You don't want to overdo it, but you need to get these muscles loose whenever you can." She replies.

I grunt as she hits a particularly tight spot. My neck rolls on my shoulders and my eyes close. I breathe through the massage, basking in her working her magic.

"Touchdown! That's what I'm talking about!" She cheers at the TV screen.

"So I take it you're into football?" I chuckle.

"Yeah, I guess you could say that."

"A girl after my own heart."

She falls silent behind me, her hands faltering for a brief second. I shove popcorn into my mouth to keep from saying anything else. I don't want to make staying here anymore awkward than it already is.

"How about steak for dinner tonight?" She says into the silence.

"Sure, I'll take whatever. Beggars can't be choosers."

Her hands pause and she shifts my shoulders so that I look at her. Our eyes lock and she narrows her gaze at me. I know what's coming. She has said it a million times since I've arrived.

"You're not begging for anything. We need to have dinner. I'm asking for your opinion," she says. "If you want something else you can say so. We don't have to have steak."

"Steak is just fine," I say, giving her a crooked smile.

"You know, I have tickets for a game next week. Do you think you would be up to going with me?"

I'm stunned by the request. It's just one more thing I can't repay. However, when I turn to look in her hopeful eyes, I wouldn't dare tell her no.

"Sure, I guess. If it's not putting you out or anything."

"Not at all. I already have the tickets. My father was supposed to go with me, but he has a business meeting out of town," she says.

"In that case, sure. Why not?"

She returns to massaging my back and we both get into watching the game. I don't know how long we sit there before I finished the bowl of popcorn and she stops the massage. Actually, I don't know how much time passes because I wake up to a different game with my head in her lap.

~B~

Allison

I wanted to get up to make dinner. However, when Roark fell asleep resting against my lap, I couldn't bear getting up to disturb him. He looked so peaceful in his sleep and his body needed the rest. I dozed off for a moment myself.

Now, instead of the steaks I had planned to make, I'm searing off some salmon. It's faster and probably healthier. Not as hearty a meal as I would've liked to help fatten him up, but it will do.

"Do you need any help?" He asks as he comes to the kitchen.

"No, I'm fine. But you can keep me company if you like."

"Sure, I can do that." He says as he takes a seat at the kitchen island.

The kitchen falls silent as I sauté the green beans in garlic butter. It's nice to have someone to cook for. I'm so used to being here by myself when I'm actually home.

Roark gets up and moves to the refrigerator. He takes out the wine I have chilling and pours a glass. Instead of drinking it, he places it down beside me. I turn to him and give him a bright smile.

"Thank you," I say.

"No problem."

He moves back into the living room and shortly after, music begins to fill the house. A tranquil ambiance takes over the space. I find myself swaying to the music and humming along to the lyrics.

Roark gets plates from the cabinet, placing them where I can reach them. He then starts to set the table. My smile grows. I take a sip of wine and watch him over the rim of my glass.

He turns and our eyes lock. My cheeks flame and I drop my head. His handsome face does this thing to me that I can't explain.

"I thought I told you to keep me company, not set the table," I say, as I cut off the burner and prepare our meal to move to the table.

"You take care of me. I'll cater to you. It's the least I can do," he replies.

I move over to the table with our food and place it down. Roark pulls my chair, causing me to look up at him and smile. I shake my head.

"What am I going to do with you?" I say.

"At the moment, have dinner with me," he replies.

His words come across as if having greater depth, but I shake the thought off. I take my seat before I embarrass us both. He already has reservations about being here. The last thing I want is to seem like some perv offering him a place to stay in exchange for his body.

Get it together, Allison.

"How about playing some cards after dinner?" I ask as he sets my glass of wine on the table and takes his own place. "Or are you too tired?"

"To kick your butt? I'm definitely game," he chuckles.

"Big talk, lots of big talk," I tease back.

"I'll back it all up too," he says in that sexy voice and I swear my tummy flips.

Lord, help me and my dirty brain. He did not mean it like that.

Although, when I look across the table, I'm not so sure anymore. His eyes seem hooded, but distant as if he's seeing something before him.

Maybe it's time I use my vibrator. Yup, that should help me stop tripping.

"Are you going to eat?" He says, grabbing my attention.

"Yeah," I say. "Just lost in thought."

"You go in to talk about the private practice tomorrow. Don't you?"

Wow, he really does listen to me. I nod, as I chew, taking a moment to think about what all awaits me in the morning. My life feels like everything is about to change.

"Yeah, that's tomorrow," I say on a sigh.

"Cool, so I won't keep you up too long kicking your ass in cards," he teases.

"Whatever."

We finish the night much the same way. Like two old friends, reconnecting and having a good time. At least, that's what I have to remind myself repeatedly.

CHAPTER SIX

Thanksgiving Joy

Allison

I've been nervously cooking since this morning. Nervous because my entire nosey family will be coming to my house this year for Thanksgiving. Not to mention a pair of blue eyes that have been watching my every step.

He has offered to help several times, but I won't allow him to. He needs to be on the couch resting. Too bad he won't take his butt to said couch. Maybe I could breathe if he did.

Ro—or Roark as he has asked me to call him—has gained all the weight I remember him having back in the day and then some. All in the most delicious way. I walked past his room yesterday to see him powering through push-ups and flipped out.

He chuckled and waved me off. According to him, he feels better and promised he wouldn't push too hard. From the way he's filling out the white dress shirt he's wearing today, he's been pushing hard all right.

"I don't know why, but I never thought about you in the kitchen," he says out of the blue.

"Really? Why not?"

We've fallen into a routine. Roark either hangs with me and it's like we're two old friends catching up. Or he just stares, watching me.

It's not in a creepy way. Most times I get the feeling he's just lost in his thoughts. I can understand that. I get that way sometimes.

"I don't know. When we met you were doing big things. I just pictured you with a lawyer or doctor husband. You know, with a staff in your home cooking for you," he replies.

I laugh. "That's the life my parents would love for me to have. Me, not so much." I shrug.

"That's sort of hard to believe," he says.

My brows crease and I look up from the cabbage I'm stirring. He seems to be looking at me more closely. His gaze causes me to shift on my feet.

"I don't know why you would think that. I've never been into titles and all of that. I want someone I can share a happy life with, not a profession. Trust me, if you knew some of the shit doctors do in the hospital, you'd understand why I'm not running to date one," I scoff.

"Seriously?"

"I have stories. I'd have you peeing in your pants with some of them," I say.

"We'll have to get to those," he says with that sexy crooked grin. "So what is your boyfriend like? Is he coming tonight?"

My cheeks heat. I turn for the pies in the oven just to get a reprieve from is eyes. When I turn back he's still watching me.

"No, he won't. I don't have a boyfriend," I say softly.

"Again, hard to believe."

I roll my eyes and place my hands on my hips. I hate it when people act as if I need to have a man in my life. I've been doing just fine without one.

"Why? Because every woman needs a man. Give me a break with that. I've watched guys walk all over the women I love. I'm in no hurry to have my heart broken or my bank account emptied.

"When and if I find the one, it won't be based off of anyone's standards but mine. I hate that during this time of year, I have to deal with daddy shoving the next potential partner down my throat. Or my mother having a nice *boy* she wants to invite to dinner.

"It's the reason I had dinner here this year. That way I can choose the guest list, and that does not include a hook up for me. Shoot, I don't even have my shit together." I push a hand into the top of my curls.

My chest heaves and my ears burn. I didn't mean to go on that rant. My family just drives me crazy with trying to marry me off. When in all reality, I don't know what I want.

"I'm sorry," Roark says.

"Don't be. I'm the one that should be apologizing. The holidays stress me out. Can I tell you something?"

He nods at me tightly. I remember that night we hung out. We talked for hours at that party as if no one else were there.

"I took a leave from work before I was suspended—"

"You were suspended? Was it because of me?" He asks, concern covering his face.

"Yes and no. Not really."

"You're lying. You do this thing with your lips when you lie. I saw you do it a few times when you were talking on the phone earlier," he says, narrowing those blue eyes at me.

"It wasn't because of you. It was because I didn't follow protocol. My boss had it out for me in the first place. If it weren't for my father, he would have found a way to toss me out on my ass a long time ago. I'm too good at what I do for his racist, sexist liking," I huff.

"Why would you put everything on the line for a stranger?"

"You're not a stranger."

"You didn't know that when I was bleeding out and all filthy on that street," he tosses back.

"I'd do it again," I shrug and move on. "Anyway, I took a break because I don't know what I want anymore. Seeing what I thought was a glamorous life up close…I don't know if I want it. It's not glamorous at all.

"The long hours, the politics, the everyday fight because I'm a black woman. I'm just tired. The love is gone. Honestly, saving your life was the first time I've felt alive in an OR in so long I can't remember."

"So what do you plan to do?"

My face crumbles. "I don't know. Maybe find a smaller hospital. I've been offered to go into a private practice. I want all the things that my parents don't want for me."

"At the end of the day, it's your life," he says.

A warm smile comes to my face. "You know you told me that ten years ago. You're the reason I went for it all. Not just becoming a doctor, but a surgeon."

"We said a lot that night. I remember having a lot of beers too," he chuckles.

"Yeah, I remember that too," I give my own laugh.

"I had no idea a girl your size could down so much alcohol and still stand. I knew from that point, we'd be friends," he says.

"Yeah, I thought so too, but what happened?"

I get the words out just as the doorbell rings. Roark stands as if he has a fire lit under his ass. I'm a bit disappointed.

"I'll get it," he calls over his shoulder.

~B~

Roark

Thank God for the save. I didn't want to tell Allison that she dodged a bullet. I wanted to kiss her so bad that night, but Carter pulled me aside and got in my ear. He reminded me that someone like Allison was way out of my league.

He'd been right for once. I was so wasted I just wanted to get out of there after that. I lucked out.

I saw the girlfriend of one of my buddies from the shop. She offered to take me home. I was so in my feelings about it all, I don't remember if I told Allison goodnight or not.

I push that memory behind me. Me walking away that night was the best thing I could've done for her. She deserves better than what I would have given her.

"Ro?" India says in confusion when I open the door.

"Hey, India."

"What are you doing here? Wait…oh my God! You were the guy at the hospital. I knew I knew you from somewhere. Holy—," her words cut off as she looks down at the cute little girl in her arms.

"Can we take this inside? My buns are freezing off out here." Erica says.

The Myers sisters are all gorgeous in their own way. I don't blame my cousin for being crazy over India. As she walks in, a little boy follows her, holding her free hand. My eyes shift between the two kids.

Family.

I think I understand Allison's words from that first night, a few weeks ago. I'm even more curious now. My cousin has been in the papers a lot in the last week. Rumors about his career, a new album, and drug use.

I shake my head. Like Allison said, none of my business. I'm still working on me.

Allison's parents walk in behind the sisters. I don't miss the seemingly disapproving look that's sent my way by her mom. Her father looks more curious than anything.

"Good evening," I say to them both.

"Hello," her mother speaks first. "Where is my daughter?"

"She's in the kitchen, ma'am," I reply.

Mrs. Myers reminds me a bit of Tina Knowles. With a Toni Braxton in the nineties cut. Her face softens just a bit, but I still see the caution in her eyes.

She looks to her husband, drawing my attention to him. He looks like he's about to interrogate me, but thinks better of it as his wife reaches for his hand and gives it a squeeze.

"I'm Allison's father, Jackson Myers," he says.

"Yes, sir. I know who you are. My step-father was a good friend of yours," I reply.

His brows shoot up. He searches my face, probably trying to make a connection. His eyes remind me of Allison's. She takes more after her father's dark brown skin and brown eyes than her sisters. India looks more like her mother and Erica falls in between.

"You said, was?" He says.

"Yeah, my step-father was Henry Fox," I reply.

His face takes on that pitied look I hate so much. His hand comes out for mine. I take it and give him a firm shake.

"Your step-father was a very good friend of mine. You must be Roark. He was very proud of you. Talked of you as if you were his own. I'm sorry I was never able to meet you before…I'm sorry for your loss," he says.

"Thank you. It's been a long time," I say tightly.

"Yes, but something like that can stay with you for a long time. I was so sorry I couldn't make it back for the funeral," he replies.

I nod, not wanting to dwell on the topic. Seeming to understand, he nods and turns toward the door. A guy I hadn't given much attention to stands waiting.

He has a smile on his face and a bottle of wine in his hand. Allison's words from earlier come back to me. This must be this year's offering.

My jaw tightens at the thought. Jealousy rises as I look over his suit and tie. He looks like the type of guy Allison should be with. Clean cut, wealthy, a smooth brother with his shit together.

Yet, her protest earlier says otherwise. Which is why I allow myself to relax and push down my feelings.

"Roark, this is Stanley Burkes. One of my fine, up and coming attorneys," Mr. Myers says proudly.

"Nice to meet you," Stanley says, reaching out his hand.

I take it but I shake harder than I need to. He winces a little but tries to return the grip. It ain't happening.

"I'm sorry. Are you a friend of Allison's?" Stanley asks.

"This is the young man that saved her life," Allison's father says.

"Oh, wow. I was very sad to hear about all of that. I'm glad you were around to help out," Stanley says tightly, as he looks me over.

"Yeah, I'm glad I was able to save her," I say pointedly.

"So, Allison invited you as a thank you?"

This motherfucker.

He wasn't invited at all. Not by Allison, that I'm sure of. I see that look on his face. I'm used to it.

White trash.

I hear the words in my head as if he says them out loud. I've been called worse. I know what it's like to be the black sheep.

"Well, I have a lot to be grateful for. Why don't we all get settled in? Stanley, come meet Allison," Mrs. Myers says before I can answer Stanley's question.

I flex my hands at my sides as they walk away. Taking a calming breath, I go to follow them. Only India appears, stepping in my way.

"Your piercings. That's why I didn't recognize you. The brow ring and earrings are all gone. But I guess they don't let you keep stuff like that in prison," she says lifting a brow.

My body stiffens again, but that mischievous smile I know her for appears.

"Relax, Ro," she chuckles. "Thanks for what you did for my sister. I know you were locked up for some bullshit. I just wish...I wish I could have done something to help."

"Looks like you had your own thing going on," I say nodding to the two kids she walked in with.

"Yeah, your cousin is a dick. He's good for giving up on people. He had his head up his own ass when everything went down with you," she says.

"I'm not his responsibility," I shrug her words off.

"That's bullshit and you know it. He knew Carter was an asshole and none of us ever wanted anything to do with him," she replies folding her arms over her chest.

"Yeah, wish I would have followed that instinct."

Her eyes soften and she moves in closer. "It's good to see you. You look good. If you need anything, and I mean anything, you let me know. Not just because of Allison. You're family," she says with a smile.

"Thanks. Your sister has done more than enough for me."

"Not even, you don't know Al," She snorts. "She's going to go to the ends of the earth to find a way to help you."

"I'll be leaving soon. I think I've overstayed my welcome already," I say, looking into the living room where Allison is talking to Stanley.

India turns to follow my gaze. She shifts into me, nudging me with her hip. A glance down at her reveals she has that mischievous smile back in place.

"Dude doesn't stand a chance. Al would chew him up and spit him out. He's too busy kissing my dad's ass to see he's out of his league. Now, you," her eyes roll over me. "You're the kind of guy my sister needs."

She winks at me and walks away leaving me stunned. My stare moves back to Allison. From the tight expression on her face, I don't think this Stanley guy is going over so well. She looks my way and her eyes are almost pleading.

Even with the distress in her features, she's gorgeous. The blue satin dress hugging her curves gives her an elegant look that reminds me she's much too sophisticated for me. I don't have half of what Stanley has to offer.

"Dinner is ready. I just need to set an extra place," Allison announces. "Hey, Roark would you mind?"

"Sure, I can help," I say, moving to join her.

~*B*~

Allison

I'm so annoyed I could scream. I can't believe my parents pulled this. I don't know why I'm surprised.

Thank, God Roark was able to talk me off the ledge. If he hadn't I would have lost it. He's been a saving grace all evening.

Taking the seat next to me before Stanley could. Keeping the conversation off of me. Even going as far as helping me in the kitchen whenever I needed a break from my mother.

"Come have a walk with me," my father says, as everyone else has a lively conversation in the living room.

I nod and follow him to the coat closet. He helps me into my coat before putting his on. Looping my arm through his, he leads us out of the door. But not before I spot my mother watching with a smug grin on her face.

I let out a heavy breath as we walk outside. I know what's coming. I've been dreading it all night.

"Your mother wanted me to talk to you," he starts.

"Yeah, I'm sure," I mutter.

"Don't get grumpy on me so fast. I want to talk to you, but your mother and I have very different opinions," he says.

"How so?" I ask cautiously.

"I like Roark. I was concerned when your mother first told me you took him in, but I can see he's a nice young man. He just walked into some trouble," he replies.

"I don't know what happened. We knew him when we were younger. He had his own businesses and was doing so well for himself," I muse out loud.

"From what India told me this evening, he took the rap for his no good step-brother and things went south from there."

"Seriously?"

"India doesn't know all of the details, but she knows he went to jail thinking he could keep the other young man out of trouble, but Roark seemingly didn't know the depth of the trouble his step-brother had gotten himself into," he replies.

"That's terrible."

"Yes, I feel terrible about it. India had come to me to get a friend out of trouble, but you know all the things she had going on then. I was so angry with her I refused to listen," my father says with so much regret.

"Don't beat yourself up, dad. You didn't know what was going on, and as bad as all of that had to be for him, it still led to him saving my life," I say.

"Yes, yes, it did. That's probably selfish of us both."

"Yeah, it did sound that way after I said it," I admit. "I want to do something to help him. I had to fight with him just to get him to take the clothes I bought. I've been wracking my brain for ways to do something that can help out."

"What about a go fund me or something?" Daddy suggests.

"That's actually not a bad idea," I say excitedly.

"I'll donate when you have it up. Not only is he a nice young man, but he also saved one of my treasures. I don't know what I would have done if anything had happened to you," my father says, with emotions clear in his voice.

"So what are we doing about mommy?" I ask.

"You leave your mother to me," he kisses my temple. "You're helping a friend, not ending the world."

I laugh and wrap my father's waist for a hug. We continue our walk and talk about football for the remainder of the stroll.

CHAPTER SEVEN

Go Fund Me

Roark

"Ugh, this is the worst part of being the host," Allison groans, as we stand in her kitchen.

It's going to take a while to clean this place up. I unbutton my cuffs and roll my sleeves up to the elbow. This I can do. It will make me feel better to contribute in some way.

"Why don't you go rest? I'll take care of all of this," I say.

"No way, it would be easier if we do it together. I wouldn't dare leave all of this on you," she says, side-eyeing me.

"Fine, we'll work together. As long as you don't say I can't help at all," I tease.

"Fair enough," she says with that stunning smile and glowing brown eyes.

She kicks off her shoes and moves towards the sink. I love how short she is next to me. It's sexy. Closing my eyes, I remind myself not to go there.

"Wash or dry?" she asks.

"Whichever you prefer, I'm good." I shrug.

She hands me that towel and shifts to the sink to turn on the water. We fall into a comfortable silence as we work. I don't notice I'm staring until she looks up at me with a brilliant smile.

"What?" She asks, as her eyes dance over my face.

"Nothing," I reply and focus back on the dishes.

Shaking her hand dry, she reaches for my forearm. I turn back to meet her eyes. She opens and closes her mouth a few times.

"Thanks for tonight. Running interference and everything. You didn't have to, but I appreciated it," she finally says.

"I don't know what you mean," I say and wink.

She laughs, but I can see more in her eyes. As if she didn't say all she wanted to. I give a warm smile.

"Can you believe they brought that guy here?" she says, turning back to the dishes in the sink.

"What? He was a catch," I say, holding back my laughter.

"Then I can give you his number," she says, looking at me to roll her eyes.

"He gave you his number?"

"Yup, not that I plan to call." She replies and shrugs.

"Why not? He seemed nice."

"Ugh. Don't you start. Did my mother rub off on you?" She teases. "I don't know. He wasn't my type."

"What is your type?" I say the words before I can clamp my mouth shut.

She turns to lean her hip against the sink. Her arms fold across her chest, drawing my attention. I force my eyes back up to hers. She's looking up at the ceiling before meeting my gaze again.

"I like my guys down to earth, you know? Not afraid to make things happen, but not chasing anyone else's approval either. I want a guy that makes me feel safe. Someone that listens to me, someone I can listen to.

"Oh, and sorry, but that guy was way too short," she says and laughs.

I reach behind her to turn the water off as I see it rising. Her breath hitches and our eyes lock. It's like I'm sucked into her orbs. Heat surges around us and I want nothing more than to lean in and take her lips.

"Wh...what's your type?" She breathes bringing me back to my senses.

I take a step back. My eyes dropping to my shoes.

"I don't really have one," I lie to keep from telling her that she's the one. My type in every way.

"Come on," she says, tilting her head at me. "I remember you having the most swag, back in the day. What kind of girls did you pull in, with all of that?"

I shrug. "Never the type I wanted."

Her phone rings pulling a groan from her lips. Her shoulders sag as she moves to find it and answer. My jaw works as I wonder if that's Stanley.

I pinch my eyes closed in frustration. I don't need to worry about Allison's love life. I need to get my freeloading ass out of her house so she can get on with her life.

~B~

Allison

"Wait, slow down. What are you talking about?" I say to Erica.

"There's a video. Oh my God, Allison. You had to be scared out of your mind. I can't believe what happened. You downplayed this so much," my sister cries into the phone.

"What video?"

"I'm texting it to you now," India says. "I knew Ro was no joke but damn! He was whipping ass before that punk shot him."

I tune out my sisters to watch the video that comes through to my phone. I watch it at least three times. A shiver runs through me as I'm thrown back into that night. I truly didn't know if he would survive.

"Wow," I say, as tears stream down my cheeks.

I went into doctor mode that night to save his life. Watching it now, as I'm removed from the scene…we were both lucky. The guy Roark had knocked out had come to while I was working to stop the bleeding.

He could have hurt us both or taken the car they were after in the first place. Anything could have happened. I don't even remember half of the things that I watch play out before me.

"I don't remember him much, but I'm so glad he was there for you," Erica says.

"Can we talk about how hot he is now though?" India says.

"Okay, so it's not just me?" Erica says.

"Nope, but Ro has always been fine as fuck," India laughs. "Girl, back in the day he had this swag about him. Like…damn!"

"Seriously, India?" I chide.

"Oh please. You know good and well you drooled over him when you met him. First white boy I saw you break your neck over," she giggles.

"Whatever," I huff. "I think I should use this video for the go fund me. You know, to let people see what he did for me. Make the connection."

"Wait, go fund me?" Erica says.

"Yeah, I was talking to Daddy about wanting to help Roark out and he suggested I do one. I don't know where to start but I think the video would help," I say and begin to chew on my lip.

"I got this," Erica says. "I'll have it up by the morning. With any luck, we can get this to go viral."

"That would be awesome. He's such a great guy. What happened to him was so messed up. I would love to see him get his life back," India says.

"I hope we can get enough for him to make some steps in the right direction," I say. "I want to make sure he's secure when he leaves. I think he's itching to go."

"Are you chasing him away?" India asks.

"No," I grumble. "I think he considers himself a burden."

"Mm," my sister returns.

"Whatever."

"You two are crazy," Erica laughs. "You leave it to me. I've got this. You know this is what I do, boo."

"Okay, do it. Let me know if you need anything," I reply. "Talk to you guys later."

CHAPTER EIGHT

Run-In

Roark

I wanted to be out of Allison's house weeks ago. It's going on a month now and I still haven't made the decision to go. One of the things keeping me there is the look Allison gets in her eyes when I start talking about moving on.

I hate seeing those sad eyes and knowing I'm the one that made them that way. We've talked about my limited options and knocked around ideas. She's sparked something this morning.

I'm feeling a bit optimistic after our talk. One of my biggest draws to being a barber was the art. On the inside, I got into tattooing a little bit, after some of the guys saw some of my artwork.

With a new idea in my head, I decided to come see an old friend to ask some questions. After all, I'm not as ashamed to come around these parts. I've put on plenty of weight while staying with Allison.

I started getting in little workouts for strength and to curb the calories I've been intaking while she feeds me constantly. I don't know if it's from her being a doctor or what, but Allison has this nurturing quality about her. I'm trying not to get so used to it.

She makes it her business to care for me. Like today, she insisted on giving me a ride here. I told her I could manage, but she wanted to drop me off and said she'd pick me up in an hour.

"What's on your mind, bro?" Drex asks.

Drex owns a tattoo parlor in Queens, right on the edge of Long Island. We met a long time ago when I was young and hardheaded. There are a lot of people in my past that I've chosen to leave there.

Looking around this place, I wonder if I should reconsider that and call in a few favors. I shake that thought off. That's not what I came here for. Besides, it's been way too long. I know nothing of that world anymore.

"I was thinking about getting into the ink business. It's not like the barbershop. I can get the license with my record. I don't know…I thought I'd come run the idea by you and get some feedback," I reply.

"Dude, I've told you for years I think you would be an amazing artist," he says.

"Yeah, but I never thought about putting down my clippers back then. Never had a reason to."

"Yeah, that shit was fucked up. Carter should have manned up."

"I did some work while doing my time. I think I'm ready to pursue this," I say rolling right over his words.

He nods as his eyes narrow in on me. I don't give a fuck about Carter and I don't want to talk about him. I want to get my life back in order. I want to be able to repay Allison for all she's done.

"Actually, getting licensed in NYC versus out on the Island is a big difference," Drex says thoughtfully and sits back. "If you plan to tat in the city you can get licensed online for around a buck thirty.

"Now, if you're looking to do it in LI, you're going to need an apprenticeship. You need a thousand hours under an approved artist. It costs around a buck to apply for the license in LI. Either way, I've got you if you want this."

My shoulders sag. I didn't think about where I want to do this. I hadn't thought that far ahead. My wheels start to turn.

I have so much to figure out. I'll need the money for the license either way. That's something else I need to consider. If I wash dishes somewhere for a bit, I can get that money up.

"Bro, if the money is an issue, I'll put it up for you. Listen, I'm expanding again. Czar wants to invest in a new shop in your old stomping grounds. I could use a guy like you to manage the place. We'll get you those hours," Drex offers.

Czar.

Yeah, Drex is still deep into that world. I don't know if I should go knocking on those doors again. I pull a hand down my beard.

"I see that look. You're wrong, bro. Everything has changed," Drex says to my silence.

"Can I think about that? I might take you up on the offer to mentor me though," I reply.

"Sure, I'll give you the site to get more information, but I hope you do think about it. Dude, the big boss likes you. You're one of few that has always known who he is," he says.

I narrow my eyes at him, but I don't pry further. I'm not ready to open that bag. Carter's dad introduced me to a shadowed world that blew my mind when I was younger.

"Like I said. Things changed."

"I hear you. Look, I'm going to head out. My ride should be back," I say.

"You have a number I can reach you at?"

"Nah, not yet. You can give me yours," I say.

He nods and stands to jot his number down for me on a piece of paper. My mind is racing with a million thoughts. I have so much to figure out.

"I'll walk you out," he says, as he hands me the paper. "I need a smoke anyway."

We head out front, joking around about old times. I don't see Allison's car as I scan the street. I lean back and settle in to wait.

"Aw, fuck," Drex groans at my side.

I turn to him in confusion. When I follow his glare, my face morphs into a scowl of rage. Carter is sauntering his ass across the street with a smile.

"Bro," he croons as if nothing ever happened.

"You've got to be fucking kidding me," I mutter.

"Ro, come on, man. Why do you look like you don't want to see me?" He says and tilts his head to the side.

I'm vibrating with so much fury, I can't speak. I want to break his neck. My jaw works as my mouth waters with the taste of the ass whipping Carter is begging me for.

"Walk away, Carter," Drex says.

"Oh, come on. I'm hurt you weren't the one to call me and tell me that my big bro was out here paying you a visit," Carter says.

"Maybe that's because I don't fuck with you," Drex spits back.

"Aw, come on," Carter grins.

"This is all just a game to you," I seethe.

It's not a question. It's the truth. I'm just seeing it once and for all for what it is.

"Look, I feel bad for how things went down. I didn't think they'd give you time for it, bro. You were squeaky clean. You know all of dad's connects. I thought you'd call for help," Carter says.

"You're an idiot. You don't just call for favors from your father's friends, you dumb fuck. Where's my money? How the fuck did you lose my house?" I snarl.

"A couple of jobs went bad and I needed the money. That shit is gone." He shrugs as if it's no big deal.

It's enough to make me snap. I charge him, raining blows down on him. I punch him in the face so hard his head rocks back. I'm not satisfied with the connection, as Carter stumbles dazed from the attack.

I break his body down before tossing an uppercut to his chin. He hits the floor like the piece of shit he is. I glare down at him with a sneer.

"You took my life away with your carelessness. You knew that shit was in the car and you said nothing. You let me take the fall and bled my fucking life dry," I bellow, as my chest heaves.

"I thought I could fix it. It all just got out of control," he gasps back. "I'm sorry."

"No, you're not. You're a spoiled asshole. Stay away from me. I swear you better stay away from me."

"So you're going to abandon me now?" He tosses at me.

I look at his battered face in disgust. Not able to process his words. I grab him by his collar and drag him to his feet. We're face to face, nose to nose as I look him in his eyes. I want to make myself clear.

"You abandoned *me*. You left *me* for dead. Yet, here you stand, accusing me of abandoning *you*. Carter, you always seem to slip your way out of trouble. I won't be there to take the fall for you next time.

"Keep away from me. I've already lost everything. I don't think I'll hold back from killing you next time. I'm barely there now," I say through my teeth.

"Roark?" Allison's voice grabs ahold of me.

My eyes close as I continue to vibrate with anger. I shove Carter away from me. Opening my eyes to glare at him.

His eyes are focused behind me. That arrogant smile comes to his lips. I'm ready to knock it off even before he speaks.

"So you finally went after her," he snorts. "Doesn't she know you're broke as fuck?"

I don't think about it. Allison screams my name, as I haul back and rock his ass to sleep. I turn, grabbing her arm to lead her back to her car.

He's dead to me.

~B~

Allison

I'm silent on the bathroom floor as I nurse his bruised knuckles while he sits on the closed toilet seat. The rage rolling off of him is thick enough to taste. I don't know what all of that was about but I don't think I should ask.

When I pulled up, the tatted white guy with the dreads—that Roark hugged when I dropped him off—was standing there with his arms folded, watching while shaking his head. He didn't move to stop what was going on. I jumped out of the car not knowing what to do.

"That was my step-brother," Roark says, pulling my attention from my thoughts. "I spent five years in jail because of him. I didn't think assault would be such a big deal, a slap on the wrist. Any good lawyer would get me out of it," he scoffs.

His eyes lift to search mine. I remain quiet to listen to his words. His gaze fills with pain and falls away again.

"Boy, was I wrong. He had drugs and a gun in the car. I was lucky to only get five years. I was thirty-one. Had my shit in order and I threw that all away to help him stay out of trouble.

"When I got out. Everything was gone. My house, my cars, my money. He cleaned me out. I was doing time for him and he was on the outside doing the same shit that got me locked up while he ruined what was left of my life," he says, with a bitter face.

His words continue to flow with so much hurt. I want to wrap my arms around him and hold him.

"You asked one time, what happened to me? That's what happened to me. I treated him like my little brother. I always had his back. When our parents split, I still checked on him and made sure he knew he still had a big brother.

"His dad was never the…coddling type. He gave tough love. I understood that but Carter was different. He needed to know someone cared. Turns out I cared too much," he says, his eyes fixed on his hands.

"I think what you tried to do for him was noble. It was a big lesson for you but your heart was in the right place," I say.

"I should have been franchising out my shops by now, in a big house with a wife and kids. Not homeless and hopeless," he says, lifting his eyes to mine.

"We can say where we think we should be. Then life challenges that dream. You can still have all of that. It's just going to be on a different timeline than you thought," I say softly.

"Do you honestly believe that?"

"Yes, Roark, I do. You can make this happen. That's a hell of a lot to go through. And look, you're still standing," I reply.

His blue eyes stare into mine for so long I hold my breath. I want to deny the chemistry I feel between us. Roark has so much going on. He doesn't need to add me to all of that.

"Thanks, Allison. Thanks for all of this," he says and tugs me into a hug.

His big arms engulf me, leaving me breathless. His embrace is warm and strong. He holds on like I might run away if he lets go.

Damn. I'm jealous of that wife.

CHAPTER NINE

A Little Fun

Allison

I slam the front door behind me. I'm so frustrated. This has been the day from hell.

I can't believe my mom. She called me over for lunch and that Stanley guy was there. I tossed his number in the garbage the same night he gave it to me.

If that wasn't bad enough, I got a call from Dr. Tucker, informing me that my job at the hospital is in danger. Sure, I haven't decided if I planned to return there, but this...this has me livid. I should have known my asshole boss was going to try this shit.

"You all right?" I turn from my pacing to find a shirtless, sweaty Roark staring at me with concerned eyes.

"No, I'm not all right. I'm so pissed. Do you know that lunch was a damn ambush? Then my boss—"

I clamp my lips shut. I don't want him thinking any of this is because of him. I start to tug off my gloves and coat, muttering to myself.

"You know what you need?" He says behind me.

I turn trying not to look down at his chest. Damn, he really has put on weight. He looks incredible. Muscle memory is an amazing thing.

"What do I need?" I sigh.

"A break. You think too much and you've been uptight for days. How about we go out?" He says with a smile.

"Go out?" I parrot.

"Yeah, I know this bar. They serve the best wings and beer. Did you get my text? I may have gotten my hands on a little money. I thought I'd treat you to a couple of cold ones," he says.

I did get his text, but I didn't get to read it because my mother was breathing down my neck. I was surprised he sent the message actually. He was so adamant about not taking the phone I gave him as an early Christmas gift.

I wanted him to have one after that run-in with his step-brother. It took some persuading, but eventually, he gave in.

"Oh, no. You can't spend your money on me," I protest.

"I'm not taking no for an answer. Sort of like someone I know." He gives me a wicked smile, before looking my outfit over. "You're going to need to change. The breakfast at Tiffany's look won't work for this place."

"Oh, you've got jokes?" I laugh.

He shrugs. "I'll shower and get ready. We can leave in an hour?"

"Fine, I'll be ready in an hour," I say.

~B~

Roark

"Seriously, that guy was so wasted. I thought he was going to fall out of the bleachers," Allison laughs, taking another sip of her beer.

"You're not lying. Between him and that couple that kept arguing I was surprised we were able to enjoy the game," I say, shaking my head with my own laughter.

"I know, right. It was a killer game though," she beams. "Hey, I'm going to run to the restroom. I'll be right back."

She hops from her stool and heads for the bathrooms. I can't help watching her walk away. I'm not the only man in the room with eyes on her.

Damn, she's killing those jeans.

I've thought the same thing a hundred times already. My eyes are glued to Allison's ass as she makes her way to the restroom. Those killer black heels have all kinds of dirty thoughts running through my head.

I like that yellow sweater on her. It brings out the hues in her skin, making it seem as if she's glowing. I won't lie and say I haven't looked down at the decent amount of cleavage showing.

I take a deep breath and shake my head. The night has been going great so far. We've both allowed ourselves to just be. I haven't thought about my bullshit and Allison seems less stressed since we've been here.

I'm grateful to Drex. I sent him a text with my number yesterday. He called today asking if I would cut some hair at his house. I was game, thinking it would be just his two boys.

He scooped me up not that far from Allison's. Once we got to his place, he had fifteen heads waiting for me. Fifteen at a minimum of twenty-five dollars each, not counting tips and extras.

It felt good to have clippers in my hand, doing what I love. It also made me think about my options. But tonight, none of that's been on my mind. I feel like an ordinary guy out with his girl.

"What are you smiling about?" Allison says as she leans into my arm.

I hadn't realized I was lost in thought for so long. I wrap an arm around her shoulders and kiss her temple. Her eyes sparkle when she looks up at me.

"I'm having a good time," I say.

"Oh my God, I never thought about that. This is like your first time out, right? Like, to hang with friends? Well, besides the game," She rambles.

It's adorable. We've had quite a few. I'm glad she suggested we Uber back to her place after.

"Yeah, I guess you can say that," I reply.

"I think this calls for another round," she cheers, causing me to laugh.

I flag the bartender down for two more. Allison remains pressed into my side. When I turn my head back to her I find her staring at me.

"I wanted to ask you something. What did Carter mean that day?" She says.

I groan internally. I was hoping she missed that. I still want to knock him out again for it.

"You want me to be honest?"

"Of course," she says, placing a hand on my chest.

I try to ignore how good it feels. Her palm is searing me right through my shirt. My gaze holds hers as I try to think of the best way to say this.

Here goes nothing.

"I had a thing for you. When we were at that party, I spent all that time with you because I was seriously interested. Carter tugged my ear to remind me you were a Myers girl and I'm…me," I say.

"What does that mean? You're you?"

"Sweetheart, you're so far out of my league," I reply.

"Roark?"

"Yeah?"

"Shut up," she says.

Her eyes drop to my lips. Her brows draw in. She looks up into my gaze again.

"But why did you leave with that other girl that night?"

"Jill? She was my buddy's girl. She offered to get me home since I was so wasted," I reply.

"Oh," she says thoughtfully.

I move my arm from around her shoulders, down to her waist. She steps in between my legs to get closer. We're both lost in the moment. I go to dip my head to kiss her just as her name is called out.

"Allison, is that you?"

Allison turns her head and I purse my lips in frustration. I can already taste her on my tongue. I was this close to something I've wanted for years.

Maybe it's just not meant to be.

I hate the negative thoughts that fill my head. She's been having a great time with me tonight. I've been the one keeping that smile on her face.

"Hey!" Allison sings to the two guys and three girls that just walked up.

She pulls the pretty brown skin girl into a hug. They rock back and forth with the embrace. I can see there's a true friendship between them.

"Hey, you." The blond with the green eyes says, as she looks me up and down. She was the one to call out to Allison.

"It's good to see you, Allison." The shorter of the two guys says.

My jaw works as his eyes roll over her. Allison moves out of the hug with her friend to embrace the others. The guy that spoke waits to be last. My fists ball at my sides, as their hug lingers too long.

"And who do we have here?" The blond says as she gets closer to me.

"Hallie, this is Roark, this is Hallie, Doreen, and Jocelyn. These two guys are Eric and Jeff," she says by way of introductions.

"And you are Allison's…" Hallie says.

"We're friends," I reply.

"Yeah, friends," Allison says, turning away from me.

The guy, Eric, smiles wide and moves in closer to Allison. He leans to say something in her ear that makes her laugh. I can't help the jealousy that takes over me. I turn away on my barstool.

Hallie takes the seat that was Allison's. She's pretty, but not my type. I want to get out of here. This night is leaving a sour taste in my mouth.

"So, I've never seen you in our circle. How do you know Allison?" Hallie asks.

"I'm sorry, Hallie. Excuse me," Allison interrupts, squeezing her body in between us.

I turn back towards Allison and she backs in between my legs. Staking her claim. Feeling bold and like the old Roark, I wrap my arms around her waist, pulling her back to my front.

Allison tilts her head back to look up at me. She bites her lip and has this sexy ass look in her eyes. Lifting on her toes, she kisses my cheek then moves her lips to my ear.

"I'm not about to watch her flirt with you. Are you ready to go?" She whispers.

I chuckle. "Yeah, I think that's best before I punch this dude for eye fucking you."

She laughs, kissing my cheek again. My cock twitches in my pants. It's been too long since he's had any attention. With Allison's ass pressed against me, my mind wants all the things it shouldn't.

"It was good seeing you guys. We're going to head out," Allison announces, grabbing her things.

She reaches for my hand to lace her fingers in mine. I look down at our intertwined grasp and my mind has a million questions.

Shut up. Just go with it.

CHAPTER TEN

Letting Go

Allison

Roark said I needed to kick back and relax. I think I want to kick back and do more than relax. It's been a long time since I've had sex.

Riding in the Uber—tucked under his arm, engulfed in his cologne—I know what I want. If I heard him right he had a thing for me back in the day. Which means he should be down for what I have in mind.

I feel this connection between us. I know he does too. At least, that's what it feels like the look in his eyes is saying.

I unlock the door and turn to face him before walking into the house. He looks down at me with desire and curiosity in his. I reach for the zipper of his coat and pull it down. My hands go inside and become consumed by his heat.

"I don't think you should go to your room, when we go inside," I say.

"No?" he says leaning in to place his forehead to mine.

"No," I shake my head. "Have you ever wanted to just let go?"

"Sometimes," he replies.

"Good, tonight, I think we both should let go. I had a crush on you, Roark. I think I still—

Before I can get the words out he crushes my lips. His assault consumes me with a blaze. I open my mouth and his tongue dives in. I moan and a deep groan comes from his throat.

"Roark," I yelp, when he dips and lifts me onto his waist.

"I've got you, baby," he pants, pushing into the house with me in his arms.

He takes my lips again and kisses me deeply. I cup his face and take as much as I'm getting. His kisses are like fire. I want more, so much more.

His heavy footfalls carry us into my bedroom. I wiggle out of my coat and toss it away. Roark's hands go to my ass and squeeze.

My panties are soaked inside my jeans. I need out of these clothes before I combust. Seeming to read my thoughts, he starts to pull my sweater over my head.

His eyes fall to my breasts, the hungry look in them sends a shiver through me. He moves us over to the bed, where he places me gently. He shrugs off his coat before tearing his shirt up over his head and tossing it to the side.

I lick my lips as my eyes eat him up. He toes off his boots and opens his jeans. I reach to unfasten my bra, but he shakes his head.

"Don't. I want to enjoy unwrapping you," he says, his voice heavy with lust.

I nod and wait my turn, as he shoves down his jeans, revealing his boxer briefs. His thick erection strains against the fabric, demanding release. Roark moves to me on the bed and drops to his knees before me.

He takes his time looking me over as if deciding where he wants to start. His long fingers wrap around my ankle and free my left foot from my heel, before doing the same with the other leg.

"You have adorable feet," he says.

He lifts his hand to the button of my jeans and unfastens it. It feels like it takes forever for him to release the zipper and tug the fabric down my hips. His eyes remain on mine. It's almost like he's waiting for me to change my mind.

That's not going to happen. I'm so ready for this. I've wanted this man for a long time. I'll admit that to myself.

"Beautiful," he murmurs, cupping my mounds in his palms.

I push my hand into the front of his hair and poke my chest out, pleading for his attention. He dips his head and kisses the tops of my breast, moving from one to the other. He peels the cup down on the right side. His tongue lavishes my tightened peak.

My eyes roll back. His heated mouth feels so good against my skin. I cry out and tighten my grasp on his hair. He groans, reaching for my hips to draw me closer to him.

"Roark," I moan.

"Yes, baby," he replies. "You want me to eat that hot pussy?"

"Yes, please."

He tilts me back with a hand in the center of my chest. I look down my body to watch him peel my panties from my skin. He licks his lips, as his eyes zone in on my center.

His lip tucks between his teeth, causing my belly to quiver. He looks so sexy, the want in his face has me in my feelings. He lifts my legs over his shoulders and moves in with a tortuously slow pace.

"Mm," he groans as he inhales me.

My hips lift off the bed when he takes his first lick. His hands cup my thighs holding me down, as he pushes in more and devours me. I watch his blond head bob between my legs, as he holds a tight grasp.

His sounds of pleasure mix with mine. I try to crawl back away from him, but he follows me up the bed. My heart feels like it's going to burst through my chest.

"Fuck," I scream out. "Oh my God."

"You have me starving for this pussy. Stop running, baby," he demands.

My head thrashes, as he returns to his task, adding his fingers to stretch me while sending me over the edge. My body shakes with my orgasm, as my juices drip down between my cheeks. I pant, trying to hold onto the sheets beneath me.

"You like that?" He asks as he hovers over my lips.

My tongue flicks out over his mouth, tasting my essence on his. I push him on to his back and call on all my energy to follow. My eyes lock with his.

"How long has it been since you've had head?" I ask seductively.

He bites his lip and groans. His eyes narrow on me. I wait for his answer.

"Over five years," he says as his erection throbs in his shorts.

Hooking my fingers in the waistband, I tug them down his hips. I get them down to his ankles and he kicks them the rest of the way off. Settling between his legs, I inhale his scent, as I look up at him through my lashes. He smiles back at me.

I lick from beneath his balls to the front, until I get to the root of his dick. Taking a long slow trip to the tip, I savor his flavor. He releases a loud long groan that turns into a loud whoosh of air when I take him to the back of my throat in one pass.

"Oh shit," he grunts.

Yeah, I've perfected this skill. My ex used to come home whistling, knowing I would give him the brains of his life. I think I put something extra into this for Roark.

I make this wet, sloppy, and nasty. My fingers are in my pussy, while I work him with my mouth and other hand. Roark sits up on his elbows to watch. I let drool cover my hand, as I pump him. His legs are moving all over the place at my sides as if he doesn't know what to do with them.

"Damn, baby," he says huskily.

I moan in pleasure. He's the perfect size. Not too big, not too long. He's just thick enough and long enough to enjoy and relish. But there are no mistakes to be made, he's above average.

"I'm coming," he says tightly.

"Mm, then come," I say around his tip, before taking him in deep all over again.

I don't have to ask twice. He comes hard down the back of my throat. I hum in pleasure as I swallow it. Roark watches me with awe in his eyes.

"I need condoms. I want you," he says.

I climb up his body, resting on his stomach. Leaning over for the side table, I reach in and pull out a few foil packets. I toss the extras on the tabletop and bite into the one left in my hand.

His heavy dick is poking me in my back as if he didn't just come. I shift to roll the condom in place. His hands grasp my hips, as he flips me onto my back. He has my legs over his forearms as he thrusts into me.

"Roark," I cry out, as he stretches me.

He stills, looking into my eyes. He feels so good pulsing inside me. Cupping his face, I bring his lips to mine. He deepens the kiss as his hips start to move.

I whimper into his mouth. Roark doesn't hold back. He dives in, pounding at my pussy in the best way. I don't have to tell him how I like it. He gives it to me just the way I need it as if we've done this together before.

"Damn, you're so tight. Your pussy is so good, baby," he croons, looking down into my face. "I'm sorry. I know I'm slaying this shit. Tell me if you need me to back off."

I shake my head. "No, please. Just like that. It feels so good. I can take more," I pant.

"Fuck," he growls and starts to really give his all.

His stroke game is off the hook. He works in combinations that don't give my pussy a chance to recover. But those long strokes, those are my undoing.

I gush around him, as my body jerks beneath him. He dips his head and latches onto my breast and I lose my shit. I scream his name like he's committing murder. To think of it, he is.

He just rocks his way right through my orgasm. When he lets up, I think he's done. So wrong, so very wrong. He flips me onto my stomach and laps at me from behind. His strong fingers part my cheeks, as he buries his face between them.

"Oh my God," I cry.

I come beneath him again, but he's not finished. His hand comes down to slap my ass before he places a palm over my head. He uses his hips to walk my body towards the headboard. When he stops my head is tucked between my shoulders, my back is pressed to the headboard and my ass is in the air.

"You good, baby?" He asks.

"Yes," I whisper.

"Good," he says, before plunging back into me.

I use my arms to hold on to the sheets, as he pounds me into the headboard. Pulling my legs around the top of his torso, Roark puts in that work. Slapping my ass a few times while tearing it up.

Well, damn. Is it always like this?

~B~

Roark

I beat this pussy up like a straight savage. I've been jerking off in the shower for weeks with thoughts of Allison in my head. The real thing is better than I ever could have imagined.

"You like that, baby?" I ask as I slap her fat ass again.

"Yes," she whimpers, as she gushes around me.

I grasp the headboard and really start to nail her to it. I should be more gentle with her, but all I've ever known has been fucking. I've never had someone to make love to. I want that with Allison, eventually.

Although, right now, I'm fucking the shit out of her. This tight pussy is too good to do anything but. I bite my lip as sweat drenches my face. It starts to drip on to her ass.

I have no idea why that turns me on. The sight of my sweat on her skin and my cock thrusting in and out of her brown and pink pussy are driving me insane. Not to mention the sound of my hips, slapping her cheeks with each pound.

"Fuck, Allison. I want to come all in this pussy," I groan.

I think back to her sucking my cock and swallowing my seed. My groin tightens and I swell inside her. I'm not going to last too much longer.

"Please, Roark, please," she cries.

"Come with me, baby," I demand, reaching for her clit.

Her loud screams have me shuddering with my own climax. I come so hard, my scalp tingles and my chest feels tight. I've never come like this before.

"Fuck," I roar.

My head goes to the headboard, as I catch my breath. Allison wiggles free of the position I've placed her in. Shifting, I lie on my side and pull her into me. Placing a kiss on her shoulder, I inhale.

Appreciate the moment while you can. You're going to have to leave now.

CHAPTER ELEVEN

Don't Be So Sure

Allison

I sway my hips to the sound of the music playing, while I make us breakfast. I'm surprised I can do this much dancing. Although, I am sore and walked into the kitchen a little funny this morning.

I can't help the smile that won't leave my face. Last night was amazing. At some point, we slowed things down a bit, but it was just as intense.

I bite my lip, as my cheeks ache from grinning like a fool. Roark is amazing in bed. The more sex we had the more that confident guy I used to know came forward.

"Good morning," I hear behind me.

I turn to see a not so confident Roark watching me. He looks cautious and unsure. Turning off the pans, I place down the spatula in my hand.

My arms go around his waist, as I look up into his eyes. I get the feeling he's ready to bolt. I lift on my toes and peck his lips, but he doesn't deepen the kiss the way he did all last night.

"Did I do something wrong?" I ask, releasing him and taking a step back.

"No, no," he shakes his head. "I…we…I think maybe the alcohol took things too far last night."

"Is that how you feel? Were you drunk?" I ask, watching his face.

"No, but I had plenty," he says. "So did you."

"Roark. I knew exactly what I was doing last night. Over and over and over again. I think the cheap beer wore off around one in the morning. We were still going at dawn. So, yeah, drinking had nothing to do with it for me," I reply.

He runs a hand through the front of his hair and blows out a breath. My arms fold over my chest. I thought we made a connection.

"Allison, you're amazing. You have so much going for you. You don't want to start anything with me. I'm not the kind of guy you want," he says.

My face softens and my shoulders sag. I move closer and tug him forward by his T-shirt. His arms go around my waist and my lips turn up.

"Are you sure about that, Roark? I want you to be very sure giving up all of this…," I cover his hands and move them to my ass. "…is really what you want."

~B~

Roark

I stand with palms full of her ass in my hands and I'm hard again. All of that sex last night and I still want more. I crave more.

Hell, no. I don't want to give this up.

I place my chin on top of her head and release a heavy sigh. I'm not selfish, never have been. I rock her from side to side, as I think of the right words to say.

"I have feelings for you. They've been growing over the weeks. Do I want to walk away from you? No. Should I? Yes," I say.

She pulls back so our eyes meet. "Why? Why should you?"

"I have nothing—"

"You are an amazing man. I should be nursing you back to health, but you have turned the tables. You think I haven't noticed?" She says.

"Noticed what?"

"You pour me a glass of wine when I need to relax, you do the dishes after I cook. Last night, taking me to that bar so I'd forget my problems and making me laugh for hours as we got lost in that place.

"You've been catering to me like you're already my man. You listen to me, you anticipate me and my needs. You might as well be," she says with that smile in place.

Cupping her gorgeous face, I run my thumb over her lips. I war with what I want and what I know I shouldn't have. Her eyes plead with me not to run from her.

"Are you sure this is what you want?" I ask.

"I know I want you. I know we'll figure out the rest. Don't push me out. I think we have something worth holding onto," she replies.

I crush my lips to hers and devour her mouth. Lifting her, I place her on the countertop. She tugs at my T-shirt as my hands roam her curvy body.

"I think breakfast is going to be cold," I chuckle into her mouth.

"Who cares? I'll make more," she moans.

CHAPTER TWELVE

Gone Viral

Roark

Laughter spills from her lips as I bury my face in her neck. I think it's the beard tickling her, from the way she's squirming away. Allison turns from the sink to wrap her arms around my neck. I take her lips like it's the last time I'll ever get to kiss her again.

I'm still in awe of getting to do this. Having her in my arms is like a dream. It's not just the amazing sex that she makes sure I get plenty of, not that I'm complaining. Allison has a very healthy appetite and she loves taking care of her man.

Her man.

To be honest, she makes me feel like more than that. I feel like I've found someone I can grow with. Someone, I can figure this shit out with. She never makes me feel like a loser or like I've failed at life.

It's more like having my best friend in my corner, cheering me on. Which I think is why I'm frustrated. Drex has lined up cuts at his place a few more times, which I'm grateful for, but we can't keep doing that.

I need something more so I can take care of my girl. Hell, Christmas is breathing down my neck and I don't know what I'm going to give her.

I've been saving the money from the cuts. I have enough to pay for a ride to the mall and hopefully to buy her something nice. I just don't know what to give a woman that has everything and can get anything she wants.

"What's up?" Allison asks breathlessly. "What are you thinking about?"

"Nothing, I missed you today," I reply.

She looks at me skeptically. I sway her in my arms, trying to hide my worry. It fails. She sees right through me.

"You can talk to me. What's going on?" She says softly.

"I plan to take a portion of the money I've saved to start the process for my tattoo license," I reply.

Her eyes light up and her arms tighten around me. Seeing that pride in her eyes makes my chest swell. I want to see that look all the time.

Allison comes from money. My mother married into it in her second and third marriage. I've known what it's like to go without—not Allison. I never want her to either.

"That's great. Once your driver's license arrives you can start to use my car to—"

"Hold on, baby," I laugh. "I appreciate everything you've done, but I want to figure this out on my own. I'll manage a ride."

Her lips pout a little, but she nods. I can see her thinking of a way to help anyway. It's what she does.

As if shielding me is her job. While I'm grateful that she wants to and has helped so much, that shit is chipping at me as a man.

"Allison?" I say gently.

"Yes," she replies.

"You've allowed me to be your man. Now, I need you to let me figure that out. I want to take care of my girl, not have her taking care of everything for me," I say.

"I get that, but a virtuous woman holds her man down and covers his head in his times of need, while he figures things out. I hate watching you struggle when you don't have to," she says.

Damn, I love this woman. Yet, I'm six years older than her. It will eat my ass up if I don't furnish her with the things she deserves.

"I think we need to find a balance. I'm not that dude that will hand over all his control. I had to do that once in my life and I hated every moment of it.

"Being locked up takes that away. Can you understand my need to make decisions and place things in order?"

"Yes, when you put it like that," she nods, tears welling in her eyes.

I don't want to see her crying. I cup her face and kiss her nose before kissing her sweet lips. Things start to heat up quickly.

I groan when she reaches into my sweats to wrap her hand around my growing need. At the same time, I'm thanking God I found a woman that can match my insatiable drive. Shit, I need a job just to replenish the condoms that are getting low in the bedside drawer.

"No, no, no," she whimpers, as her phone rings.

I release her as she stomps her foot. She's in full pout now. Her face is the cutest, as she stares down at my sweats with lust in her eyes. Huffing, she stomps out of the kitchen for her phone.

I shake my head at her as she walks away. For the first time in a long time, I'm hopeful for the future. Piece by piece, I'm going to get my life back.

~B~

Allison

I want to kill my sister, as I see her name on my phone. I had a long day at Dr. Tucker's practice. It was thrilling and challenging. Something I think I've been missing.

"Hey, India. What's up?" I say into the phone.

"Okay...don't sound happy to talk to me," she replies.

"I'm always happy to talk to you. How are the babies?"

"Those are not babies. Those little folks are grown terrors," Erica's voice calls.

"Anyway. They are fine and asking about both of their Tee-tees," India says. "But we called for a reason."

"Yes, we did," Erica says cheerfully.

"*O...kay*," I drag out.

"It went viral!" Erica squeals. "It just exploded overnight. I can't believe what I'm looking at. We've exceeded our goal by three hundred percent and it's growing!"

"Wait, what?"

"The video of Ro saving you and getting shot is all over the internet. It's trending on all of the social media sites. People that know him, people that were patients of yours. They're all getting behind this to help," India rushes out.

"Oh my God! Really," I sob out. "That's amazing!"

"Yeah, so what do you want to do? Do you want to give him this for Christmas?" Erica asks.

"Absolutely. He's been so stressed out. This is just what he needs," I say biting my lip.

The wheels turn. This would be something of his own doing technically. He saved me and now life is rewarding him. At least, that's how I intend to explain it.

"I'll come over so we can work out the details. We don't have a lot of time," I whisper into the phone.

"Cool, I'm on it," Erica replies.

"I have a question," India says.

"What?" I say cautiously.

"Last two times I called your voice was a little breathless when you answered. Are you letting Ro in them panties?" She says.

"Good night. I love you both," I sing into the phone.

"I knew it," she hollers.

I hang up before she can dig any deeper. I have a smile on my face, as I clench my phone to my chest. I don't know how I'm going to keep this in until Christmas.

CHAPTER THIRTEEN

Merry Christmas

Roark

I'm nervous. Not only is this my first time at Allison's family's home. I had to figure out gifts for everyone and that cut into my budget for Allison's gift. I got lucky with a last minute call for Christmas Eve cuts.

"Baby, smile," Allison says, as we wait for the door to open, our hands full of gifts.

"I could've stayed at the house. You didn't have to bring me along."

"Why would I leave my boyfriend home alone on Christmas?" She says, looking up at me with a sparkle in her eyes.

She's been grinning happily all week. Her eyes have been glowing with joy this morning. It's the only reason I didn't try to back out of this.

"Are you sure this will be okay with your parents?" I ask one last time.

"Positive," she says, tipping up on her toes for a kiss.

I meet her halfway, pressing my lips to hers just as the front door opens. A throat clears, calling my attention to the person staring back at us.

Relief rushes through me when I see it's India. She has that mischievous smile in place as she waves us in. Walking into the Myers home is like walking into a movie.

It hits me hard that Allison has known a life way different from mine. The elegant fixtures and double spiral staircase are just the beginning. I'm afraid to move. I don't want to make a wrong step.

"Come on. We can put these under the tree and get some breakfast," Allison says beside me, as my gaze swings around the foyer.

I nod and follow after her to the huge tree in what looks to be the family room. There are a ton of gifts under the tree already. I wipe my sweaty palms on my slacks, before reaching into my pocket for the gifts I bought for the family.

"What's that?" Allison asks, pointing to the wrapped gifts I place under the tree.

"I got everyone something," I reply.

"I told you, you didn't have to Roark," she groans.

"And I told you I didn't feel comfortable not doing it," I say.

She purses her lips at me. Her brows shoot up when I pull a gift from the inner pocket of my jacket and place it under the tree as well.

"Do I want to ask?" She says.

"Maybe, but I'm not going to answer," I tease.

"Come here, you," she says, tugging at the front of my coat.

What starts as a small kiss deepens, my hands on her hips as I consume her lush mouth. She has my ears in her grasp, keeping me locked to her. I almost forget where we are.

"There you are," Mr. Myers' voice brings us back from our own world.

I jump back as if I'm a teenager all over again, not a grown ass thirty-six-year-old man. Mr. Myers chuckles, easing my nerves a bit. He waves us over.

"Come get some food before my little grandson eats it all," he says.

"We were on our way," Allison says, as I help her out of her coat.

She takes mine, rushing off and leaving me alone with her father. I move to offer my hand. Instead of shaking, he pulls me into a hug. I'm stunned but I return it.

"You're family, son. We hug when you're in my home. You look well," he says breaking the hug and placing a hand on my shoulder. "How's the side?"

"I'm doing well. Can't complain. Ready to get back out there to get on my feet again," I reply.

He gives me that mischievous smile I know India for. I can't help thinking that they're in on a secret that I'm not. I shrug it off as he pats me on the back.

"My door is always open if you need an advisor or anything else," he says.

"Thanks. I appreciate that."

Allison returns and snuggles into my side as we all walk to the dining area. The rest of the family sits around the table having breakfast. Erica has a sour look on her face, as some guy I've never met sits to her right talking to her.

"Looks like they've moved on to the next daughter," Allison snickers.

"Seriously?" I chuckle.

"Yup, I told my parents that we're dating. So I'm off the project list," she says.

I squeeze her side before releasing her to pull her chair. It feels good to know she has told her family about us. Not that she said we had to hide it. I just thought they would find out when we arrived today.

"Good morning," Mrs. Myers says.

She looks between the two of us, but some of that wariness has faded. Oh, it's still there. I can see it, but not as much as Thanksgiving day.

"Good morning, ma'am," I reply.

"You can call me Mrs. Myers or Edith," she says.

"Good morning, Mom," Allison says.

"Good morning, Allison. I thought you said you'd be here earlier. The twins have been eager to open their gifts this morning," Edith says.

"That would be my fault," I say.

Allison starts to laugh. "He wasn't happy with the shape up Lisa gave me yesterday. He wanted to clean it up." She tells her Mom.

"I was going to say that your hair looks different. I like it. It's cleaner or something. It compliments your face," India says. "You had me ready to start going back to Lisa. Never mind."

"Do you think you can shape up my dreads? I was thinking about cutting the sides off or something," Erica says.

"Sure, anytime. Just let me know," I say.

"Cool, I'll give you a call."

"That's right. You're a barber by trade?" Edith says.

"I was," I say simply.

I'm not sure if Allison told her mother about my record. Most people at this table know I was homeless. I'm not sure who else knows about my record other than Allison and India.

"How about we head to the family room to start sorting a few of the gifts. Everyone can pick their first gift to open, while Roark and Allison get some food in their stomachs," Mr. Myers says.

"Yay," the twins cheer, jumping from their seats to run for the Christmas gifts.

Everyone at the table laughs. India gets up to follow the kids while shaking her head. Allison pours me a glass of orange juice as her mother continues to watch the two of us.

"Edith," Mr. Myers says in warning.

She holds her hand up to stop him. I shift in my seat uncomfortably. My knee bounces under the table.

"Has Allison told you that I was a psychologist before I became a stay at home mom?" She says.

"No ma'am, but I already knew that," I reply.

She nods. Her eyes searching my face. Allison reaches under the table for my hand. She squeezes my fingers and I return the gesture.

"Traumatic events can often force two people together. Dire circumstances can cause someone to cling to a savior. I just want to make sure this isn't what's going on with the two of you," Edith says.

I go to reply, but Allison gives my hand another gentle squeeze. Her father is the one to speak up.

"And I told you to leave it be. Roark doesn't need to explain himself. I've welcomed him into our home and this will be a welcoming experience. I may not have done right by one of my best friend's child in the past, but it will not happen again.

"Roark, Allison. Eat your breakfast and join us when you are ready. If you want to eat it in the family room, you're welcome to," he says, standing up and ending the conversation.

Edith glares at her husband, but she doesn't say a word in front of us. She follows him out of the room. Erica does a slow clap once they're gone.

"Don't you want to follow them?" She turns to the guy sitting next to her.

The stunned look on his face is hilarious. If I weren't so uncomfortable and irritated, I might have laughed. Allison turns to me, once she and Erica are the only two left in the room with me.

"Are you okay?"

"Yeah," I say tightly.

"No, you're not," Erica says. "Ignore our overbearing mother. She'll never be satisfied. Sometimes I think she likes to screw us up so she can try to fix us. But she means well."

With that, Erica gets up and leaves the room as well. Allison piles a bagel and fruit on my plate. I told her that I'm looking to start eating leaner now that I've gained my weight back.

"Do you know what your father meant?" I ask.

"About?"

"He said he didn't do right by his best friend's kid."

Allison sighs and turns to her own plate. I watch and wait. My unease rising by the second.

"India went to my dad to help you when you first got in trouble. According to my dad, it was around the same time we found out India was pregnant. She and my dad fell out about a lot during that time.

"As a result, when she went to ask for help for you. My father wouldn't even hear her out," she says. "I think that's weighing on him."

"Wow."

I don't know what else to say to that. Of course, I don't hold it against him. I didn't expect anyone to come to save me. I knew the moment all hope was lost for my case.

"Erica's right. Ignore my mother. My father will handle her. He has liked you from the beginning before we were together," she says, leaning to kiss my cheek. "Let's take this into the family room. I don't want the twins to fall out and have a tantrum because they have to wait any longer."

I nod. My head filled with information. I don't have time to think any of it through, but I save it all for later.

~B~

Allison

I had already placed Roark's name on gifts that I bought for the family. I didn't want him to use his money. However, I'm almost in tears as my family takes turns opening the gifts he got for them himself.

They're simple gift cards wrapped in Christmas paper. Yet, each gift card matches the person he purchased it for. Roark had asked me all about my family and I told him little things about them.

It's clear he listened to the details. He got everyone so perfectly. A bookstore gift card for Erica. A wine gift card for Mom. I can't believe he got everyone just right.

"He's a keeper," my Dad says beside me.

I look at him and nod. My cheeks ache as I smile at him. Daddy winks at me, gesturing with his head for me to turn. I shift to find Roark holding a gift towards me. It's not flat like the others so I know he didn't get me a gift card.

I look into his blue eyes and he looks nervous. I chew on my lip as I take the gift. I'm curious, but I try to take my time opening it.

"Girl, if you don't hurry up," India huffs.

"Thank you," Roark groans.

I chuckle at them both and tear the paper away. A velvet jewelry box is inside. My brows shoot up. I know he's been making money cutting hair, but this looks like it could be a costly gift.

I open the lid of the box and gasp. It's a necklace with a heartbeat pendant. The electrocardiogram wave flows into a diamond covered heart shape. I finger the pendant with shaky fingers.

"Roark? I told you not to do this," I whisper.

"And I told you, I wouldn't feel right if I didn't. It isn't half as much as I wanted to give you, but I hope you like it," he says.

"I love it," I choke out, as I stand and throw my arms around his neck. "Thank you."

His arms wrap tightly around me. Kissing the top of my head, he holds me a little longer. It's the same type of warm hug he gave me that day I nursed his bruised knuckles.

Remembering my present for him, I break the hug and look up at him with an excited smile. Erica is already at my side handing over the envelope. I take it and hand it to Roark as I pull him to sit next to me.

He looks at me questioningly, but I wave for him to open the gift. He gives me that sexy smile and tears the envelop open. Taking out the folder inside, his brows draw in.

I wait with bated breath for a reaction, as I watch him read through. I'm not expecting the response that covers his face. Instead of the smile I was expecting, he looks at me with anger.

"Can we go somewhere and talk?" He says tightly.

"Yeah, okay," I say, as he stands.

I move ahead of him to lead the way. I start for my old childhood bedroom, optioning for more privacy. Something tells me we'll need it.

"Why are you so angry?" I ask as I close the door to my old bedroom.

He tosses the folder onto the bed and shoves his hand in his hair. His head lifts as he stares at the ceiling and blows out a breath. It looks like he's trying to rein in his temper. When his eyes meet mine again they are full of hurt and ire.

"I thought you understood how I felt. Here we are in this house you grew up in. I just sat and watched your family give you expensive gifts. That necklace…it was the best I could do and I was all right with that because I know that as soon as I get my shit together I'll do better.

"I already owe you so much and have nothing to contribute. Every night, I lie in bed with you, busting my brain to figure out how to get my life back so I can do right by you before I lose you," his breath hitches as if his last words caused him pain.

"Why would you go behind my back and do something like this?" He says with so much hurt.

"I…I didn't think this would be the same as doing everything for you. You earned that. Those people gave because they wanted to help a hero. I did it before we started what we have.

"It just exploded after. Roark, that's over six hundred thousand dollars. It's a start to get your life together, but it's not going to make all your troubles go away. You still have to make something happen with it. That's all on you," I say.

He turns from me and starts to pace. I stand quietly to allow him to process it all. I can see the war taking place on the inside of him.

He turns to me and closes the distance between us. His hand cups my jaw, tilting my head back. He crushes my lips with his and sears me with his kiss.

"You drive me crazy, but I'm in love with you. Everything I do from this day forward is for you. I promise to make every single penny count," he says, as he stares into my eyes with those intense blues.

"I love you too."

CHAPTER FOURTEEN

Staff Party

Allison

After talking with Dr. Tucker, I've been thinking about some things concerning leaving the hospital permanently. It's one thing for me to choose to leave, it's another for me to be pushed out.

With the encouragement of Dr. Tucker and a few others on the medical staff, I decided to come to the holiday staff party. Another example of how ass-backward my boss is. He had this party planned for after Christmas but before the New Year.

"We can leave if you want," I say to Roark.

Roark has been on edge for the last two hours. I know why. Dawson arrived with one of the other doctors and has been glaring at Roark since they got here.

It's pissing me off so I know Roark has to be ready to blow. He looks at me with a tight expression. It's so out of place with the tux he has on. Roark looks divine in the black tux that fits his sculpted body to a tee. He's just edible.

However, the scowl on his face screams, back off. I move into his side and he thaws a little. His lips brush my temple.

"This isn't about me. I'm here for you," he says tightly.

"Ugh, I don't want to be here," I chuckle.

"You've got this, baby."

I look up at him with a beaming smile. My hand goes to my necklace that he gave me. Again, I ask myself why I'm here. I have nothing to prove. Yet, walking away without making my point just isn't me.

"Allison, there you are," Dr. Tucker says, as she walks up.

"Hey, I want you to meet my boyfriend. Roark, this is Dr. Tucker," I say.

"If you are her boyfriend. You can call me, Carissa. I thought I work hard without taking time to myself. This young lady hasn't had a boyfriend in… See that. I can't even remember," she laughs.

"It's nice to meet you," Roark says with a genuine smile.

"Very nice to meet you, Roark. Allison, Dr. Harris is asking after you. I suggest you go make yourself known over there. I'll keep your lovely man company," she says with a teasing wink.

I laugh before kissing Roark's cheek. "I'll be right back," I say.

"Take your time," he says, kissing my forehead.

~B~

Roark

"I haven't seen her this happy in…ever. Whatever you're doing keep it up. She's a brilliant doctor. With great potential. I think she just needs to decide on what makes her happy most," Carissa says.

"She's amazing," I say with a smile as I watch Allison move right into the conversation across the room.

She looks amazing. That red dress is making a statement. So are the black heels on her feet. I can't wait to get her home and unwrap her.

"You're in love," Dr. Carissa says.

I turn to her and smile. "Is it that obvious?"

"It's written all over your face," she chuckles.

"Dr. Tucker, it's good to see you." The detective that called Allison into the hallway—that day that seems like years ago—interrupts.

"Oh, Detective Green. How are you these days?" Dr. Carissa says.

"I've told you, you can call me, Dawson," he says with a cheesy ass smile. "I'm great. Keeping trouble off the streets."

He says his last words while eyeing me. My fists clinch at my sides. This dude has been pissing me off all night. He hasn't stopped glaring at me or eye fucking Allison.

"Have you met Allison's boyfriend, yet?" Dr. Carissa asks.

"Boyfriend?" He nearly snarls.

"Yes, I'm her boyfriend. Do you have a problem with that?" I seethe.

He snorts, his eyes rolling over me in disgust. "You know. At first, I thought she wouldn't give me a shot because I'm white. Now, I see her with your white trash ass and I get it. She just has bad taste." He spits.

"Excuse me?" Dr. Carissa and I say in unison.

"What do you know about this convict?" He says to her.

"Wow," I snort. "That's ex-convict and I was wrongfully convicted. Not that it's any of your business."

"Looks like a duck...," he says, shrugging as he holds his hands up.

"You look like an ass. A jealous one at that," I say with a grin on my lips. "Wish you had my girl so you're salty? You never had a chance with me in the picture or out."

"You think you're something special? It's only a matter of time before you're back in a cell," he hisses.

"Whatever. You're tough talk because of a badge. You don't know shit about me. Get out of my face," I say.

He steps closer. "I wasn't in your face. And if you haven't noticed, I'm off duty. I'll teach your bum ass a lesson right here," he says, as we stand practically nose to nose.

I lower my voice. "I'm not here for this bullshit. Don't make me put my foot up your ass."

"Hey, hey, Dawson," Allison hisses as she runs over. "What the hell are you doing?"

"What am I doing? What are *you* doing? I told you about this guy and now your fucking him?" Dawson snarls at her.

I move Allison out of the way and get all the way up in his face. His nostrils flare and he puffs his chest out. It's taking everything in me not to knock him out.

"Go ahead. You were locked up for assault weren't you?"

"Talk all that shit to me if you want, but you better show my woman some respect. Yeah, I was locked up for assault but trust me. I'll earn the time this round for whipping your ass with my registered fist," I hiss.

His eyes go wide. Yeah, I bet that has his bitch ass attention. I'll beat the fuck out of him.

"Dawson, you're an asshole," Allison says tightly. "Babe, I've done what I needed to do here. Let's go."

I don't move. I'm not turning my back on a punk like Dawson. That's not my style.

"Babe," Allison calls.

"Whatever," Dawson grumbles and backs away first.

"I'll be reaching out to your superiors and I'll have my father do the same," Allison tosses those final words over her shoulder as we turn to leave.

My entire body stiffens. I'm even more pissed.

-B-

Allison

"Why do I feel like you're angry with me?" I say, as we step into the house.

Roark whirls on me, crowding me against the closed front door. I search his blue eyes for answers as he glares back at me. He hasn't said a word since we left the party. I could just kill Dawson for that stunt he pulled.

"Do you even realize what you're doing?" He says in a quiet calm I don't believe.

"Doing what?"

"Always coming to my rescue. Always trying to save me," he says.

"I didn—"

"So you don't see it," he cuts me off.

"Roark, you and Dawson were making a scene in front of my colleagues. Of course, I was going to try to diffuse the situation," I say.

"See, you still don't get it. It's not that you tried to diffuse anything. It was your threats to get involved and get your father involved. I had it handled on my own," he bites out.

"Sure, you had it under complete control. Threatening a member of the NYPD while having a record. Totally under control," I snap.

His head jerks back. I close my eyes knowing I just went too far. I lift my lids when I feel the loss of his heat.

He's walking into the guest bedroom, not the master that we've been sharing. I stand at a loss. I don't know what to do or say.

"Roark," I choke out.

He lifts his hand and shakes his head. Looking down at my shoes my brows furrow. I don't know what to do.

Does he have a point?

Maybe he does. When I think about my parents, my father has mastered the art of dealing with my mom. I hadn't realized that I've become so much like her. Always trying to fix people, instead of supporting them as they work things out for themselves.

I shudder at the thought of becoming that woman. I love her but she can drive you up a wall. Always fixing things, sheltering, smothering, and needing to be a caregiver without any balance.

Oh my God! He is right!

Pushing off the door, I drag myself to my room. I never realized how hard it is for me to let go. I run my OR. Being a leader is in my nature. Dr. Tucker has been instrumental in that. She has always pushed me to the front.

I control the outcomes around me on instinct. I haven't been in a relationship in so long, I haven't had to look closely at the trait. Maybe it's time I reconsider that.

I kick my shoes off and start to peel my dress off. The last thing I want to do is make Roark feel like I don't respect him or care about his feelings.

"It's more than that," I whisper to myself.

If I'm going to be in my mother shoes, I should step all the way into them. I think about Roark's time in prison and on the streets. I try to think of everything from a male's perspective. I focus on getting into his head—how he sees things.

My heart aches when it all hits me. I was wrong. I meant well but I was wrong. In all honesty, if Dawson would have placed a hand on Roark, I would have gotten in the middle.

That's not what Roark wants. That was clear in the way he moved me out of the way and shielded me. He wasn't going to fight Dawson, until Dawson spoke out of place to me.

"He needs to care for me," I whisper. "He needs to know he can. Damn, he's not asking a lot."

I drag my body into my bathroom and climb into the shower. Letting the water cascade down on me, I sag. As it warms, my muscles loosen.

I place my palms and forehead to the wall. Maybe we've rushed things. I should have allowed him time to find himself. After that first night, he tried to tell me he needs time to figure things out.

Tears roll down my cheeks. I love him, I don't want to lose him because I can't let go. I'll give him time. This time it's his move. I won't force him.

Just as I come to my conclusion, I feel heat at my back. His arms wrap around me, pulling me into his chest. He tilts my head up and captures my lips.

It's a tender kiss. As if he's asking for my forgiveness. I reach up to cup the back of his head. He deepens the kiss as his hands start to roam my body. Breaking the connection, water drips from his face.

I don't even think about my hair getting soaked. His long fingers grasp my face, as his blue eyes pierce mine. So many emotions war in his gaze.

"This is the only time you give me any type of control," he says. "If you can trust me with your body, I need you to trust me with everything else. I know what's written on the wall, but that doesn't define me. If I say I've got it, I got it," he says.

"Okay," I reply.

He ghosts his lips from my hairline down over my nose. When he reaches my lips, he hovers. My instincts are to try to complete the link and aim to bring him pleasure, but I know he's testing me.

I wait him out, bringing a smile to his face. His tongue flicks out over my mouth. Nipping at my bottom lip, he palms my breast and kneads it.

His other hand reaches into my wet hair, tugging my head back. His lips start a slow trail down my neck. He follows the path back up to my ear, leaving a path of fire in his wake. I relax into his hold and let him take over completely.

"We have to work this out because I want you. You're what's been missing from my life. I'll always take care of you, Allison. I wouldn't do anything to ruin what we have," he says.

"I hear you. I'm listening to you this time. I understand," I whimper.

"Do you, baby? Do you hear me when I say how much I love you?"

"Yes, I love you too."

He covers my mouth with his again. His hand glides down the front of my body, between my legs. I gasp into his open cavern as his fingers circle my clit, then slip inside me.

It's not rushed. He takes his time as I fight not to rock my hips and rush his pace. I allow him to bring my body to a full burn as I shake in his hold. Pulling his fingers from my pussy, he sticks them between his lips.

"The best," he croons, dropping to his knees.

I reach out for the walls, as he lifts me onto his shoulders, but I don't need to. He's got me. My head drops as the realization hits me in my chest.

Here Roark is. A man with the world against him and he always has my back when I need him. He has shown that in simple ways.

The simplest one?

Listening to me. The one thing I haven't been doing for him. Yet, here he is proving that he wants to love me if I'll allow him to. Which means loving him enough to let him do things without butting in.

"Roark."

My fingers lock into the front of his hair, as he drinks from my core. I look down to find those blue eyes on me. It's enough to send me over the edge. His head moves from side to side as his tongue dives in.

"Babe, yes," I cry out.

He starts to lift while allowing my body to cling and slide down his as he rises. Wrapping my legs around him, he presses me to the wall. He reaches for the dish we've placed in here to hold our condoms for shower sex.

His jaw is tight as he rolls the rubber over his length. When he's suited up he stares at me while he lines up with my entrance. My head knocks against the tiles the moment he drives into me.

He doesn't begin to thrust. No, he decides to call for my sanity with his hips. He starts to make slow circles as he throbs inside me.

He pins me with his stare. My heart and pussy flutter in sync. Looking through my wet lashes, I try to tell him all the things I feel.

His eyes return the silent conversation. Roark owned me a long time ago. That night at the party. I was his then, we just didn't know it.

"I never should have walked away from you," he says as if he's reading my mind, while he slowly starts to move in and out of me. "See, baby, it's not hard to give yourself to me. Allow me to take the lead."

I grasp behind his neck and roll my body against his. A smile comes to his lips. He looks down at our connection.

"Yes, but isn't it so good when we work together," I purr.

"Fuck," he hisses out, as I start to bounce with his slow thrusts. He leans in and chuckles against my lips. "Balance. That's all I'm asking for. Love me and let me love you."

"I can do that," I say.

"We'll see," he says and picks up the pace.

~*B*~

Roark

I wasn't going to come in here. I had planned to give it the night to cool off. I just couldn't let it go. She calls to my heart and soul.

I had only come to talk to her to make her understand where I'm coming from. Finding her in the shower with her shoulders shaking with her tears was too much to bear.

When I finally released her from the shower, we fell into bed snuggled together. Now are limbs are tangled and the sheets are wrapped around us. I don't think I would have slept without her beside me for the night.

"I love when we talk and you help me think things out. I'm not saying I don't want that. It's the action parts. When things need action, I want to take that action," I say as I play with her fingers.

She groans. "I had no idea that I'm just like my mother. Why didn't someone tell me sooner?"

I throw my head back and laugh. I hadn't thought about it that way. Bringing her fingers to my lips, I kiss them.

"I think there is hope for you," I say through my laughter.

"You must truly love me," she mutters.

"I was born with one purpose. To find and love you. I fucked that up once. I don't intend to again," I say and wink.

"We were young. I think we're right where we're supposed to be. Roark?" She says hesitantly.

"Yeah," I reply, kissing her lips.

"I won't make the call. But I do think you should talk to my dad about Dawson. Hear me out," she says when my face tightens. "Be proactive. Dawson has a habit of digging into my life when I haven't asked him to. Just talk to daddy. My instincts are telling me you should."

"Okay, I will," I relent.

"See teamwork," she giggles. "I love you."

"I love you too gorgeous."

CHAPTER FIFTEEN

Good Use

Roark

"How have you been, Roark? Tell me how we can help?" Mr. Myers says as I sit in his home study.

I asked him for a meeting with him and India. It's been almost a month since I received the money from the online campaign. I've been taking my time to think about my next step.

"I need to produce," I blurt out, but pause to gather my thoughts.

"Take your time. Explain what you need," Mr. Myers encourages, his brown eyes warm.

Seeing Allison in his eyes causes me to relax. I'm doing this for our future. I'm taking the action.

"My friend, Drex, has been holding regular little cut parties at his place so I've been making money during those. I've done a few tats as well.

"I've been making enough money for basics. Things like my own toiletries and giving Allison money for the phone bill. It all has me considering my options. I can't get my license to cut hair again because of my record, but I can run a business.

"I think I want to open a barbershop, with a tattoo parlor attached. I've been talking to my friend and he's on board to help out. I still have a few things to think about, but I want to at least find a property," I say looking at India.

"A commercial space. I've got it. I'll find you something with a great location," India nods taking out a notepad.

"How can I help?" Mr. Myers offers.

"I'm not sure. I know there are ways for me to get around owning the shop, but my heart is in having clippers in my hands. I never should have put my life and career on the line for my knucklehead step-brother.

"I'm innocent, sir. I want to get my life back. I hope that someday I'll be able to ask for your daughter's hand. Right now, I don't feel comfortable doing that. But that's my end goal. To have Allison as my wife, a family of my own, and my business.

"Those are the things that make me, me. You said to come to you for advice. I'm here for that advice," I say.

Mr. Myers sits back in his chair, his eyes locked on me. I'm nervous inside, but I don't let it show. This is what I want. Allison and I have been working through our differences. She's been trying to let go and I've been more patient when she can't seem to.

To make things work we're finding a balance. These are my next steps to getting the life I want. The one that should have been mine a long time ago.

"India, why don't you go start on that search?" He says, not taking his eyes off me.

I swallow hard. I don't know what he's thinking. For all I know, this could be his breaking point. It was one thing for his daughter to play with me. It's another thing for her to marry me.

India gets up and leaves the room, closing the door behind her. The clicking sound of the latch rings ten times louder in my ear. I stay stock-still waiting him out as he sits quietly.

"Did you know that Frank and Henry were good friends?" He says, lifting a brow at me.

"My mother's second husband? He and Henry were friends?" I say.

"Yes, they were very good friends. That's how your mother met Henry," he says.

"I had no idea," I reply in confusion.

"Henry was probably not the man you grew to know him as. His connections are just as deep if not deeper than Frank's. I know that world was not what Henry wanted for you but in this case...I think your answers lie in calling in a few favors," he says pointedly.

"Are you saying this to me as a judge or as a friend," I say cautiously.

"Make no mistakes. I uphold the law. I've honored my seat, but I've made friends along the way. You will find that things have changed. It's a lot safer and cleaner to be a friend of the families now," he replies.

"Yeah, I keep hearing that," I say and sigh, pulling my hand down my beard.

"From what I know. Someone at the top has a fond spot for you. You've impressed him at some point. He was not happy to see that video. I'm sure he would open his arms if you asked for help," he says.

"I don't need his money. I need to clear my name."

"I said nothing about money. You asked for a solution to clear your record. I've given you the best one. I would have a lot of red tape to go through. I get a sense of loyalty from you.

"It would be safe to say you wouldn't testify against your step-brother to clear your name," he says with a knowing smile.

I fall back in my seat. He's right. I should want Carter to rot in jail, but that's not me. I'm not going to snitch.

It wouldn't be smart given the connections I've made in my past. If you snitch on one, you'll snitch on others. That's the way it will be seen.

"I see what you're saying," I huff.

"Take your time. Think about it. I'll be here for whatever you need."

"Thanks," I reply.

"Have you had anymore run-ins with Detective Green?"

"Nah, haven't been to his side of town, though," I say.

"I doubt you will, even if you choose to head out that way. His first mistake was talking to my baby out of turn. I don't take kindly to people trying to embarrass the man that put his life on the line for her either.

"I hear he hasn't been happy with his desk job," he chuckles.

"I appreciate you handling that for me."

"Anytime. Wasn't a problem at all. It was my pleasure. And son?"

"Yes, sir."

"When you are ready, I'll have my blessing waiting," he says with a smile.

CHAPTER SIXTEEN

Ro's Back

Roark

If I'm going to get back to me, I'm going to get back to me. Which means I have some adjustments to make. I'm not sure how Allison will feel about what I'm about to do, which is why I brought her with me.

Her eyes are bright and expectant as she looks around Drex's shop. It's just hitting me how different we are. Allison doesn't have a single tattoo on her sexy body.

I, on the other hand, have a chest full and have been toying with the idea of sleeves and a full back piece. Eventually, I want to have a full shirt.

"I think I want one," she says, bouncing on her toes.

Wrapping an arm around her waist, I tug her into my side. I peck her lips and smile. She's so cute. Her eyes are the brightest I've ever seen.

"How about you think about what you want. I'll do it for you when you're ready," I say.

"I was thinking about getting one tonight," she says and bites her lip.

"I'm not letting any of these guys touch your body and I left my things at home."

"Roark...seriously?" She gasps.

I shrug my shoulders. "Yeah, I'm serious as fuck."

Her eyes search my face before she bursts into laughter. I palm her ass and squeeze. Dipping to cover her lips.

When I break the kiss, she stares up at me with a dazed look in her eyes. Drex walks into his private room and I shift my hand from her ass to the small of her back. I wish we had just a few more minutes to ourselves.

"You ready to bring the old Ro back, bro?" Drex asks, rubbing his hands together.

"Yup."

"So the lip and brow?"

"Nah, I'm giving up the lip," I say as I watch Allison. "Did the hardware I ordered come in?"

"Sure did. I have it here. Two earrings and one nose. Those piercings still open or you need to reopen them?"

"I'm good on those," I reply.

Allison stands with her mouth hanging open. I brush my lips over hers and wink. Her mouth turns up into a huge Grinch that stole Christmas smile. I suck my lip into my mouth to keep from laughing.

"Oh my God. You have no idea how sexy I used to think your piercings were," she says.

I brush her hair out of her eyes. She's been letting the top grow longer. I love it when it's like this, giving her a sultry look.

"Used to think?" I lift a brow.

"Get your sexy ass in that chair," she shoves at my chest.

I reach for her, pulling her into my lap. Drex works around her in my hold to pierce my brow. He also puts in the nose ring and earrings for me.

Allison cups my face and kisses me. Her eyes are lit as they bounce around my piercings. I lift my unpierced brow in question.

"You're the old Ro. The guy that told me to follow my dreams until I found my happiness. I'm resigning from the hospital. Dr. Harris called me with an offer I couldn't refuse. I'll be his second in command covering three hospitals here on the Island," she says.

"Baby, that's amazing! Wait, that's a good thing, right?"

"Yeah, it is. More responsibility, but the funding I'll have access to and the advanced research programs, I'm completely stoked about it," she says.

"When do you start?"

"I'll return in six months. I didn't want to rush back. I took time for me. I know I was heading for burn out," she says.

"So it sounds like we have something to celebrate," Drex croons out. "My bro is back and his lady's doing big things."

"Yeah, she is. Drinks on me."

CHAPTER SEVENTEEN

Panic

Allison

"Ro," I moan.

Sweat is dripping down between my breasts as Roark's palms my mounds pinching my nipples. We've been at it for hours. I've returned to work and this is the first time in two weeks that I had two days off in a row.

"Don't stop, baby. You feel how hard you make me?" He groans.

I ride him like my life depends on it. Our sex life has taken a huge dive. I think we're both trying to make up for that. Looking at Roark beneath me—his muscles flexing and working, the red in his cheeks, his sweat covered face—it all reminds me that he's alive.

This amazing man that I almost lost as he bled out in my arms. He draws me baths and rubs my feet during the limited times he gets to spend with me. He has adjusted to my crazy life in the last few weeks as if it's always been the norm.

"Roark, baby, oh my God," I cry out as he plants his feet in the mattress and thrusts up into me.

"You feel me? Damn, you feel so good," he says, as he lifts to pull a nipple into his mouth.

Always catering to me. He has proven a man of his word. He takes care of me. I come home to warm meals. When I'm too tired to feed myself, he feeds me.

He takes me to work and picks me up so that I'm never driving on the road tired and alone. Even though I now work so much closer to home. He installed blackout shades so I can sleep without the sun waking me.

"Yes, yes, yes," I cry breathlessly.

And this. He brings my body more pleasure than I can ask for. I don't know if it's because we haven't had sex in a few weeks, the music playing in the background, or just something else that has shifted between us, but this feels like the best sex we've ever had.

"Damn," he hisses, flipping me onto my back.

He fists the sheets at the sides of my head and rolls his body into mine. His face is tight with lust as he looks at me in wonder. From the look on his face, he's thinking the same thing I am.

I wrap my legs around his back and bow off the mattress. One of his hands goes to my waist, gliding around to my backside. My eyes cross and roll into the back of my head.

"Ro," I whimper.

"Come, baby. I'm not...going to...last. This shit is too good...Fuck," he groans in between pauses, fighting to get his words out.

I feel the moment he explodes inside me. My eyes widen. It's so hot and leaves me with a sensation I've never felt before. I know right away there's no way there's a barrier between us.

He thrusts a few more times proving my point. I know what it feels like when I come and he pushes through it. This is way more than just my essence gushing around him.

His brows crease. I watch as he pulls back and looks down at his length. The condom is there, but its torn in half.

"Holy fuck," he says, his voice filled with panic. "Shit. I didn't feel it break."

He lifts to his knees and shoves his hand into his hair. Anxiety is clear across his features. I sit up, reaching for his face. My lips gently press against his.

"Babe, it's not like we don't have each other's test results. Relax, it's fine," I reassure him.

"It's not fine, Allison. More than an STD can be a result of me coming inside of you," he says.

"And I would be so happy to have a baby with the man I love," I say softly.

His eyes meet mine and soften. He grasps me by the back of the neck and pulls me in for a kiss. It's a tender, loving connection. He places his forehead to mine.

"One day I do want babies. I'm just not sure now is the right time. You just started a new path in your career and I'm still getting my life in order—"

"My career would be fine. This would be a great time for me. I'm turning thirty-one this year. I'm not saying we have to start actively trying. I'm just saying don't panic about this. Relax, Roark," I say.

He nods, pecking my lips. Worry lines still crease his face, but he doesn't protest. Instead, he gets up and goes into the bathroom. After a few minutes, he returns with a warm cloth to clean me up.

Again, taking care of me. My exhausted body grows heavy and I pass out with thoughts of a little Roark in my arms. That wouldn't be a bad thing at all.

Our baby would be loved and cared for.

-B-

Roark

I pull her sleeping body into my arms. My mind is racing with so many thoughts. A baby is the last thing we need to think about.

India just found me a property that's perfect. Actually, it's one of my old shops. It just hit the market. It's like divine intervention because every other place has been wrong somehow or the deal fell through for some crazy reason.

It's time for me to make a decision. I can have the shop open by the end of the year, but I need to decide if that will be as the owner of a barbershop or a silent partner that never touches a pair of clippers or a client.

My hand moves to Allison's belly. She snuggles closer in her sleep. I blow out a breath.

"Time to man up, Ro," I huff to myself.

"Huh?" Allison says in her sleep.

I chuckle. Her light snores tell me she's answering me in her sleep. I kiss her temple.

I'll get this right.

CHAPTER EIGHTEEN

Calling in Favors

Roark

Damn, now I can truly say I've never been this nervous in my life. I told myself I'd make the call and see if this was even an option. I expected to be told yes or no.

Instead, I was invited to a meeting with four of the most powerful men in the world. Once I became open to this option, I started asking questions and found out a lot has changed while I was locked up.

I wipe my forehead and fix my tie. Allison was invited to join me, but I was relieved she had to work. I'm not so sure I'm ready to introduce her to this world. It's clear her father knows a whole lot, but I want to feel this new order out for myself.

"Why do you look so nervous?" Czar chuckles, patting my shoulder. "I remember you being a tough guy back in the day."

"Man, I was young and dumb. I didn't realize what I had to lose," I blow out a breath.

"Yeah, love will do that to you," he grins. "Make you grow and want to do things right. Relax, you're family. I was surprised you didn't get into the ring to get back on your feet."

"Nah, too much rage. After getting out," I shake my head. "I would have had blood on my hands. I wasn't in the right head to fight."

"Makes sense. You always did think with your heart," Czar says patting my cheek. "It's why LaSalle likes you."

The elevator opens just as he says those words. We step off, but I'm not expecting the reception I receive. LaSalle Locatelli, Uri Donati, Logan O'Brien, and Misha Krupin all stand before me with four women at each of their sides.

Women that look as lethal as I know these men to be. La Bella Mafia. That's their name on the streets. These must be the four queens. I've heard there are more. Wives of the new underbosses. All dangerous in one way or another.

The dark skinned, blue-eyed woman next to Uri is the first to speak. She moves forward and circles me. Placing an arm on my shoulder, she speaks in Italian.

"Questo ragazzo ti ha fatto guadagnare soldi? Gli darei un calcio al suo sedere allampanato," she snorts.

"It was only a few fights, but all knockouts," I reply. "As for kicking my ass. From what I heard you'd give me a good fight, but I think your husband would shoot me before we got a good round going. So I'd probably just let you win."

Everyone laughs easing the tension. She turns to face me, patting my cheek, then she winks at me. There's something cold in the depths of her eyes that confirms the stories.

"Ah, you understand me. Yes, the boys will like you. I'll bring them to the shop when it opens. You will cut my sons' hair. I'm Valentina Donati. You can call me, Val," she says before turning to saunter back to her husband.

"I have never seen a white boy with a shape up that clean. You cut your own hair?" The woman next to LaSalle asks.

"Yes, I work with all types of hair. My girl only lets me clean her up now. Her stylist is just for styling her length but I keep her shaped up," I reply.

"The doctor?" She says, narrowing her eyes.

"Yes, she's a surgeon," I say.

I don't hide the shock on my face. I never told LaSalle more than the fact that I was seeing someone. I hadn't even given Allison's name.

"I know all. You wouldn't have gotten next to my husband without me knowing every detail of your life," she says with a smile on her lips. "Next time, bring her along."

She turns to kiss LaSalle's cheek as his eyes sparkle with amusement. He turns from me to kiss his wife. I feel like I should look away but watching the power that rolls off the two of them is awe-inspiring. I've never seen anything like it.

When the kiss ends, she whispers something to him. He nods with a smile. Turning to look over her shoulder at me, LaSalle's wife speaks again.

"I am Tasha. My son sent you a message. It's time to buy the ring. She will say, yes. Don't put it off. Others need you to follow through."

With that, she turns to the other three women and nods. They all kiss their husbands in parting, done with interrogating me. I stare after the four women walking away dressed in all black with red bottoms on their feet. A shiver rolls through me. I feel like I just survived the firing squad.

I stand confused. I'd been warring with whether I should buy Allison a ring and propose sooner rather than later.

A voice in the back of my head has been telling me that Allison will say no because I still have nothing. I haven't told anyone about that. It's been me and my thoughts.

"Looks like you're the family barber now," LaSalle chuckles.

"Da, wife wants you cut my hair. You bring tools?" Misha asks.

"They're in the car," I nod.

"Good," he nods folding his arms over his chest. "You go get them."

I nod. I'm always prepared. Before I can turn to get my things, LaSalle speaks again.

"Bobby and his wife will take care of your problem. Paige will push your licensing through as well," LaSalle says. "Uri, you can pull strings with the business permits and a construction crew to get him up and running?"

"Done," Uri replies simply.

"My sister-in-law will step in to help ya with the tat shop. Drex is not right for ya," Logan says. "He needs to fix his shit."

"Well, that settles it," LaSalle says, walking over to pull me into a hug. "You're family. Never take this long to come to me again. Capisci."

"Understood. Thank you," I breathe feeling like my knees will give out.

I have my life back!

CHAPTER NINETEEN

Thank You

Allison

Roark has been in such a good mood in the last few months. I don't know what he has been up to. I've been so busy with work it's hard to keep my eyes open long enough to have our long talks.

I'm also working on keeping my hands off and letting him do his thing. I know when he's ready he'll tell me what's going on. I trust him to handle his business. Which it seems he has been doing.

I bite my lip as I watch him across the table. This restaurant is gorgeous and the food has been delicious. I've been tempted to ask a few times if this place is really on budget.

Keep your mouth closed, Allison.

I've been chiding those words all night to keep from saying anything out loud. Roark looks happy. Something is definitely different about him.

I tilt my head to the side as I take him in. He has on a grey blazer and blue button down shirt. A blazer and button down I didn't buy for him. The shirt has his eyes doing amazing things to my belly.

They are sparkling with happiness and bright with confidence. A confidence that wasn't there two or three months ago. My gaze drops to his lips and that sexy, cocky smile makes my nipples tighten.

"You're nasty," he leans into the table to whisper to me.

His voice sends a shiver through me. It wraps me in its silk and drips over me like the warm syrup he licked off my body this morning. My ears heat just thinking about that scene on our kitchen floor.

"What are you talking about?"

I want to kick myself when my voice comes out huskily. Yup, I just gave myself away. Not sure if I'm that ashamed, though.

"I can see your thoughts in your eyes," he whispers, his eyes dropping to my breasts. "And your body."

"Lies, all lies," I tease.

He reaches across the table and runs the backs of his fingers up my forearm. Goosebumps rise, shadowing the trail he makes. I shift in my seat.

"I know your body better than you do. I bet those panties are soaked and wet for me," he says, as he watches my tongue dart out to wet my lips.

"Maybe, but that's something you'll have to find out," I purr, leaning towards him so he can get a better look down my dress.

His eyes drop exactly where I want them. They darken. My smile turns up higher.

"Take them off," he commands.

I look around the restaurant then back at him. He can't be serious. Granted, we are at a table off to the side in its own corner. The tablecloth will probably offer a bit of a shield, but he can't mean for me to take my panties off here.

"You're not getting your dessert until I have them in my hand," he says with a cocky grin.

My mouth falls open. He's serious and I can officially say that my panties are wetter than a dishrag. My logical mind tells me not to peel my panties off in the restaurant, but the naughty part of me that loves the way his eyes have darkened with lust eggs me on.

I scoot to the edge of my seat and reach under the table. Easing my dress up, I reach for my panties and hook my fingers in them. I take them off slowly, not breaking our eye contact.

He sits back in his seat, watching with all of that swagger I remember from when I first met him. My breath hitches. Pulling the fabric from my feet, I ball them in my hand.

Roark places his up turned palm on the table. Reaching for his hand, I place the panties in it. He wraps his fingers around my hand, holding it in place. I shiver and squirm in my seat.

"Please enjoy." The waiter's voice pulls me from my focus on Roark.

The waiter has a beaming smile on his face as he places a plate before me. I follow his pointed look down to the plate. My brows thread in the center of my forehead.

"Open it, baby," Roark says squeezing my hand he's still grasping, before releasing it and taking his prize.

I reach for the envelope resting on the plate. It's not the apple tart with caramel sauce that I ordered, but it has piqued my interest. When I open it, the folder from his Christmas gift is inside.

I look up at him. I hope he's not trying to give me back that money. All of it belongs to him. He should have well over the initial six hundred grand I initially handed over. Emails poured in with more people wanting to support.

"Just open it, Allison," he says.

I flip the folder open. Within are papers, not the ones I had placed inside for his gift. I lift them out and read the first one. It's a New York State barber's license with his name on it.

"*Yes!*"

I scream so loud everyone in the restaurant stops to turn and look at us. My entire face heats. My ears burn hot. You would think my team just ran the game winning touchdown.

Roark covers his mouth as he laughs. Tears fill my eyes. I know how much he loves to cut hair. This means the world to him.

I pull out the other document to find a deed. I bounce in my seat not caring about the people watching us. I silent scream and dance in my seat.

"How, babe?" I squeal.

"India helped me find a place and close the deal. It's actually one of my old shops. The owner was about to lose it. I got it for a steal. After talking with your dad, I called in a favor for the license. My record has been wiped clean," he says with a blinding smile.

"Fuck yeah," I whisper-scream and pump my fist. "You so deserve this, babe. I'm so happy for you."

"I don't think I was half as happy as you are," he chuckles.

"Are you kidding me? You should be," I say excitedly. "I think we should go home to celebrate more privately."

He lifts his pierced brow at me and bites his lip. Raising a hand he gets the attention of the waiter, rubbing his fingers together to signal for the check. There's that swag again.

I watch him watching me. The waiter places the billfold down on the table. I reach for it.

"I want to treat you. This is all so amazing," I say.

"Nah. Those days have come to an end. I've got you. Just like I promised. I got my shit together. Now, I'm going to spoil you the way you were born to be spoiled," he says.

He pulls three hundred dollar bills from his wallet and tucks them into the billfold. I pull a face and nod. Okay. What am I going to say to that?

My man's got this.

"Allison?"

"Yeah?"

"Thank you."

~B~

Roark

I sit with a grin on my face. Allison insisted I sit in the living room and wait for her. Not just sit but sit in the armless chair from the dining room.

So I'm waiting for her to come back out of the bedroom as I sit here. I don't know what she's up to but I can only imagine. I loosen my cuffs and roll my sleeves up to my elbows.

Shifting in the chair, I throw my arm over the back. A glance at my watch tells me she's been in there for twenty minutes now. My head lifts when music starts to fill the room. "Dance for you" by Beyoncé floats through the air. I lift a brow and my smile grows.

Only for my jaw to drop, when Allison steps out in red fuck the shit out of me heels and a black leather outfit that barely covers the essentials as it crisscrosses her body. Her skin is glowing as if she bathed in oil.

"Fuck," hisses from my lips

I'm instantly hard as a rock. My mouth waters and my scalp tingles in anticipation of how hard I know I'm going to come. When she starts a slow strut—pausing to dance and roll her hips, before sauntering closer again—I lean towards her. She keeps up this torture as she makes her way to me.

When she gets to the edge of the area rug I'm in the center of, she drops to her knees and starts to crawl. She looks up at me through her lashes, her hair falling into her right eye. I pull a hand down my face, it's the only thing I can do not to fly out of this chair and flip her onto her back.

Instead, I sit back and watch. My smile is in place while my eyes devour her. She stops a foot before me and rises on her knees. Her body rolls, as she slowly drags her hand down the center.

I shake my head. I love this girl. She's the only woman that has ever made me feel like this. I shove a fist in my mouth and shake my head, when she rolls off her knees onto her ass, then back onto her shoulders.

Her ass is facing me. Jiggling in all its glory as she pumps her legs in the air like she's slowly peddling a bike. When she starts to clap them cheeks, I bite back my smile.

She rolls out of that move and starts to crawl to me again. I spread my legs as she moves in between them, placing her hands on my thighs. Staring at me, she beckons me closer with her finger.

I lean in but she denies me the kiss. She places a finger in front of my lips, hers only inches out of my reach. Her tongue peeks out as she rises.

I'm so under her spell, I follow with my gaze. She rocks her hips from side to side. My hands grasp her sexy waist, bringing her into my lap. She comes willingly.

It's a trap. She starts to grind against me driving me insane. I'm close to coming in my pants. I try to capture her lips but she backs off. Not letting our mouths connect.

Sitting back in my lap, she peels the strap on her right shoulder down, fully exposing her breast. I groan when she lifts her mound and dips her head. Her tongue circles her nipple and it's my snapping point.

Cupping the back of her neck, I take over. I crush her mouth and consume her with my hot kisses. Her fingers lock in the top of my hair as she clings to me.

Releasing her, I reach for the front of my dress shirt and tear it open. Buttons fly everywhere but I don't care. Allison's small hands slide up my chest, pushing my shirt from my shoulders.

Her head dips so she can lick my tats. I grab her ass, dragging her into my erection. I thrust into her as she grinds and traces my ink with her tongue.

She lifts her lust filled gaze to mine. "I want you," she purrs.

Reaching behind her back she pulls a condom from seemingly thin air. I grab it and tear into the pack with my teeth. Allison releases me from my jeans shoving them down my hips, I lift my ass to help her.

I get the condom on in record time. Allison slides down onto me before I can move out of the way. My fingers dig into her back as she starts to dance on my cock.

"Yes," she cries out.

Her hips sway and swirl, beckoning my soul from my body. I palm her breast and wrap my mouth around it. She loses it. Her hands go to my shoulders as she powers through the buildup I feel tightening in her pussy.

"Give it to me, baby. Just like that," I groan.

I don't let her chase it alone. We're going to break this damn chair. I lift to my feet and bend my knees as I support her. Her cries and screams pierce the air as I bring her down on my cock over and over.

"Damn, Ro," she sings.

I lick from between her breast up to her chin and nip it. She shivers once, twice, and a third time. I know I have her.

"Come for me, baby."

She does, just like a waterfall. I feel her dripping all over me. Allison unwraps from around me, dropping to her knees. Pulling the condom off my throbbing length, she covers me with her mouth.

"Ah, shit, Allison," I hiss tightly.

My leg starts to shake as drool drips down her chin. I was already close. When she takes me down her throat the second time, I can't hold back.

"Fuck!" I bellow as I explode into her mouth.

My knees give and I fall to the floor with her. Lying on my back to catch my breath, I pull her on top of me. Kissing the top of her head, as she snuggles into me.

"What was that?" I chuckle, when I can speak.

"My thank you," she says softly.

"For what?"

"Being you. Exactly what I was waiting for."

Damn, I know the feeling.

CHAPTER TWENTY

A Home

Allison

This Christmas has been one of the best. Being with my family and Roark this year was just what I needed. Life has been hectic juggling all of my new responsibilities.

I was glad I could get the day off. Not that I haven't been praying all day that I wouldn't get called in. It's been quiet and I've been on cloud nine.

"Where are we going?" I say to Roark as he passes the exit for the house.

"Santa's not finished with you just yet," he replies.

"What are you up to, Roark?"

"Relax, woman."

I laugh and shake my head. Since opening the shop he has been so happy and carefree. I still can't believe he got his record cleaned.

I don't think he would have been happy doing anything else. Behind a chair is where he belongs. He truly loves what he does.

I reach to brush my fingers over his sideburns and beard. My man is always sharp. God, he is a beautiful man and I love him.

"I think your mother might be coming into the shop for a piercing," he teases.

"Over my dead body. Oh my God. She asked you a million and one questions. I think my mom is a lowkey freak," I laugh.

"Did you see your father's face though?" he chuckles and peeks over at me.

I palm my face. "Yes, when she asked about the belly ring," we say the last part in unison and really start to laugh.

"Baby, I thought it was just me," he says.

"Nope, I caught that one too."

He reaches over to place his hand on my thigh after turning into a street I've never been on. We're not that far from my parents' house. I sort of know the neighborhood.

There are beautiful houses all around us, but not too close to one and other. I look around curiously. Surely, he can't be going to cut hair at this time of night on Christmas day.

He pulls into a driveway and parks. I look around at the beautifully lit trees on the property. It's festive and grand at the same time.

Roark gets out of the car and rounds it to open my door. I step out and look at him questioningly. The lights are all off in the house except for maybe the entryway.

"What are we doing here?"

Instead of answering, he pulls me close and kisses me breathless. My toes curl in my ankle boots and I cling to his pea coat. When he pulls away his blue eyes shine at me.

He grabs my hand and starts for the front door. I'm too dazed and winded to ask any more questions. I follow his lead up the pathway.

When he turns to me, he has a brilliant smile on his lips. I cup my hands in front of my mouth and blow on my fingers. It's cold out here. My brows crease as I look at him expectantly.

"Damn, I didn't think this shit through enough. It's cold as fuck out here," he mutters seemingly to himself.

"Roark, what's going on?" I laugh while bouncing to keep warm.

He pulls me into his arms and starts to rub his hands up and down my back. I look up at him, following the wide range of emotions running across his face. His eyes search mine just before his mist a bit.

"Ro, you're scaring me," I say, cupping his working jaw.

"I remember the first time I saw you. You were this young bright-eyed girl. It was like the world revolved around you. I had to be like twenty-five. I wasn't sure if you were even legal," he chuckles.

"A few months later, we were at that party. Everything I thought about you when I first saw you was right. You were smart, gorgeous, and funny as fuck. Only six years younger at that. You were everything I wanted.

"I grew up thinking I'd never amount to anything. Things had just started to change my way of thinking. I was just finding my success. So when that bug was placed in my ear that you were from a wealthy black family and my white trash ass could never have you, I believed it," he pauses to look away and swallow his emotions.

"Every time I'd see your sister, I'd want to ask after you. Seeing her with my cousin. I wondered if she was just the rebellious sister or if I honestly had a shot. By then, you were in medical school and didn't have time for parties or even me. Trust me, whenever one came up I'd ask if you'd be there.

"Never in a million years did I think I'd be standing here with you. Especially not when I was dirty and starving on the street," he reaches into his pocket. "Last year, you gave me a home for Christmas. This year is my turn."

He holds a set of keys up in front of my face. I look at them in confusion. Taking them in my hand, I look from the keys to Roark. Then, it clicks. I gasp and shake my head.

He can't mean…

I rush around him for the door and fumble with the keys. I push the second one into the lock and turn. The knob turns and the door pops open.

I stumble inside with tears streaming down my face. I take a few more steps and my breath whooshes from my lips. The foyer rivals that of my parents'. I'm in shock.

The large chandelier draws my attention up. I stare at it in awe. This doesn't make sense.

"Roark…how?"

He doesn't answer, causing me to turn. My hands fly up to cover my mouth. Roark is on one knee holding up a ring box. My eyes are drawn to the marble floors. Glowing against the tiles before Roark is the words, will you marry me, written in lights.

"Marry me, baby. Let's finish our story right. No one walks away this time. I want you and you want me. Be my wife," he says, through his own emotions.

"Yes," I choke out and nod frantically. "Yes."

He stands and rushes me, lifting me into his arms. I bury my face in his neck and sob. I still have so many questions but I'm so happy I could burst.

Placing me on my feet, he slips the ring on my shaky finger with his own trembling hand. When my eyes meet his blue ones, I'm lost. The depth of love I see there fills me completely.

"I love you," I whisper.

"Not as much as I love you," he returns. "I just want to give you everything you deserve."

"About—"

"It was a gift. Some friends overheard me talking about proposing, but waiting to get you the house next year. They made me promise to propose today so I could give you their wedding gift. Da quattro regine alla mia regina. From four queens to my queen," he explains.

"Wait…you let someone buy this for us? For me?"

He throws his head back and laughs. "Baby, trust me. Your new friends are not ones I want to say no to. Besides, I don't charge the men in their families for cuts. We'll even out someday."

I look around the house, then back at him with a raised brow. "You sure about that?"

"Yeah, I'm sure about that. Lots of hair to cut in those families. We're good. We're set for life," he croons.

"In that case, thank you and Merry Christmas," I say seductively before I step back and start to peel off my coat.

He starts out of his own with a smile. "Lots of rooms to christen, baby," he says, wiggling his brows.

"We can take our time. We have the rest of our lives," I reply.

Roark pauses, his eyes misting again. "Yeah, we do," he says, walking up to me to cup my face. "Welcome home, baby."

Wedding Bells

Roark

Another year. I can't believe it. I look at my fiancée and my mind is blown. Allison is glowing. We haven't told the family yet. We're waiting until the wedding. Just a few more weeks.

It's been hard to hold the secret in. I want to shout it to the world. I'm going to be a father. This time it was a conscious decision that actually placed my seed inside her belly.

Although, I've been grateful for that condom scare. It was the push I needed to take action and ask for help. Help that didn't come with the types of strings I thought it would.

If anything I've gained family and loyal customers through my connections. Because of LaSalle and my extended family, I've opened another barbershop in the city, my third.

I laughed my ass off the day good old Detective Dawson Green walked into my shop. He looked like he was going to piss himself as Misha glared at him. Apparently, he never did let go of his hard-on for me. Allison was right.

Bobby got wind of it and LaSalle invited Detective Green to the shop to let him know who he was fucking with. Green walked in to find the mayor in my chair getting a cut. While the police commissioner laughed and chopped it up with Uri.

The four kings showed their power that day. The governor walked in not long after Green with a gift for me and my fiancée to celebrate her newest promotion. Detective Dawson stood with rage in his face right before Lasalle waved him into the back room.

My record is squeaky clean, the way it should be. Dawson left with the understanding that it would remain that way. He also knows to back the hell off.

Life has been good to me since that Halloween night when I thought it was all going to end. Every Thanksgiving since, I've been humble and thankful. That night reset my life on the right path.

"Why are you looking at me like that?" Allison says from the accent chair she's curled up in.

Our new home suits us perfectly. A little of her and a little of me. I couldn't ask for more.

"You're beautiful. I just can't believe you're pregnant and we're getting married Christmas day," I say shaking my head.

"We could have gotten married on Halloween," she teases.

"Fuck out of here," I chuckle.

She bursts into laughter. She tried talking me into that shit. It wasn't happening. Probably the one time I didn't give her, her way.

"You know when the baby comes you can't have so much hatred for that day," she says with amusement in her voice.

"One of the worst and best nights of my life, but when the baby arrives that will be a reminder of all the best parts," I croon, getting up from my seat on the couch.

I lift her from the chair and sit in her place, pulling her into my lap. With a kiss to her temple, I wrap her in my arms. She snuggles into me and sighs.

"I want this for my sisters. I think this wedding is getting to them both," she says thoughtfully.

"Could that be because of the guest list?" I murmur.

"Nope, I haven't said a word," she says.

"*Allison*," I groan.

"What?"

"Baby—"

"Roark, I know what I'm doing," she says.

"Yeah, being your mother again," I huff.

"Whatever," she says, turning her face to me to pout.

How can I be annoyed with that face? It's how she gets me every time. I sigh and let the topic go. When Allison wants something, Allison gets it.

We fall silent for a while. My smile grows as I look around our home. Life definitely didn't happen the way I thought it would but it turned out exactly how I wanted.

"We turned into a power couple," Allison laughs, breaking the silence.

"Yeah, we did. Who would have thought? Giving a homeless man a home for Christmas would've turned into this."

ACKNOWLEDGMENTS

Happy Holidays! Merry Christmas! I hope this book greets you with happiness and newfound joy. I wanted to write this one for a while. I was excited to get to finish it. There are three more books in this series that I hope to publish next Christmas and during the holiday season. Blue is just taking a break this year. LOL

Thank you so much for your support. It means so much more than you could ever know. You guys are my book family. Thank you for the emails, messages, and well wishes. I want to thank everyone for their patience. You never know the walk someone is taking and when you guys come out of the blue (no pun intended) at just the right moment it's a godsend.

There are a lot of things coming. Some old friends and some new. Let's see what the year brings as I continue to open my heart and mind to you awesome readers and friends.

And we know I'm not going to close without thanking God. All praise are due. If you knew my story, you'd give Him His glory. I thank God for my blessings, those received and those yet to be seen. I will continue to allow him to use me and this creativity he gave me to share. Thank you, Lord! Let's get it!

On to the Next!! *We might just take another visit with Kitty, Rage, and the gang. Who knows?*

ABOUT THE AUTHOR

Blue Saffire, award-winning, bestselling author of over thirty contemporary romance novels and novellas, writes with the intention to touch the heart and the mind. Blue hooks, weaves, and loops multiple series, keeping you engaged in her worlds. Every word is meant to have a lasting touch that leaves you breathless for more.

Blue and her husband live in a home filled with laughter and creativity, in Long Island, NY. Both working hard to build the Blue brand and cultivate their love for the arts. Creativity is their family affair.

Wait, there is more to come! You can stay updated with my latest releases, learn more about me, the author, and be a part of contests by subscribing to my newsletter at

www.BlueSaffire.com

If you enjoyed A Home For Christmas, I'd love to hear

your thoughts and please feel free to leave a

review. And when you do, please let me

know by emailing me at TheBlueSaffire@gmail.com

or leave a comment on Facebook
https://www.facebook.com/BlueSaffireDiaries or Twitter
@TheBlueSaffire

Other books by Blue Saffire

Placed in Best Reading Order

Also available....

Legally Bound

Legally Bound 2: Against the Law

Legally Bound 5.5: Legally Unbound

Brothers Black 4: Braxton the Charmer

My Funny Valentine

Broken Soldier

Remember Me

Brothers Black 5: Felix the Brain

Coming Soon...

Road to Whatever Series (Perfect for Me): Ideal For Me Book 2

Brothers Black 6: Ryan the Joker

Brothers Black 7: Johnathan the Fixer

Other books from Evei Lattimore Collection
Books by Blue Saffire

Black Bella 1

Destiny 1: Life Decisions

Destiny 2: Decisions of the Next Generation

Destiny 3 coming soon

Star

www.ingramcontent.com/pod-product-compliance
Lightning Source LLC
Chambersburg PA
CBHW060741180626
46819CB00001B/57